I054496

With Love

and

Peace

Chocolate

*Book has been handcrafted from cover to cover,
including the watercolor illustrations by Carolee*

A Reason To Dream

Original copyright © 2010

Copyrights © apply accordingly: All rights reserved
by the author. No part of this book may be reproduced
or transmitted in any form or by any means, electronic
or mechanical, including photocopying, recording, or
by any information storage and retrieval system, without
the written permission of the author.

Copyrights © are owned by "The Carolee Collectables."

ISBN: 978-1-947573-07-9

Library of Congress Catalog number: 2017950119

The Carolee Collectables
Printed in the United States of America
www.crystalsforkids.org

Carolee O'Neill,
http://books2c4kids.com

Acknowledgements

To all my friends and family who willingly gave of their time to edit the stories of my twelve books; patiently taught me computer jargon; shared their computer skills with Adobe InDesign and Photoshop; and guided me through the copyright, ISBN and barcode maze. I couldn't have done it without you.

iv

A Reason to Dream

Dedicated to David,

whose courage and laughter
taught me that no matter how difficult
things seem, love is always on the horizon.

To:

_____

_____

From:

_____

_____

A Reason to Dream

Index:

A Reason to Dream

Index

The Story

A tumultuous process of dealing with a devastating disease is the impetus for this couple to learn to live one day at a time. Avoiding the thoughts of how the future will unfold, the heroine buries her fears in chores as surges of adrenalin ravage her heart. Sleeplessness accompanies her nights, and exhaustion fills her days. The hero struggles to maintain his dignity, as he refuses to accept any change in his life and death story. The system further complicates the journey as hospice policies conflict with decency, leaving them to feel unsafe and forced to deal with incompetence. Eyes tear as they refuse to succumb to the temptation of turning away from God. In spite of this traumatic roller coaster ride, they hang onto the unraveling threads of life through heartaches, tugs of war and, yes, even laughter.

The story gives hope to anyone who encounters a difficult situation that cannot be avoided. In addition, helpful coping techniques and pertinent Bible verses are offered in the appendixes.

A Reason to Dream

Prologue

A haunting memory pierced my heart as I sat by Canyon Lake, Arizona, in the Superstition Mountains. There wasn't an escape from the past, yet my mind convinced me so. Perhaps the silence of these majestic mountains would provide an answer, or at least some peace. I stared at the horizon. The sunlight played leapfrog over the crests of waves, as hues of blue and brown journeyed toward the rocky bank. The chilling waters of the napping shoreline bathed my feet as I remembered friends whose hearts attempted an answer, but whose voices reflected that nothing would make a difference. Time would heal the pain—they claimed—time.

Thoughts of the past and present flitted through my mind as I watched the light being reflected on the gentle waves. A devastating disease doesn't care about time. It captures the mind of the survivor, planting visions of distortion forever. If only I could cry, wash away the pain, but tears don't come, only numbness. A distant speedboat insulted my silence, sending swells crashing noisily against the shore. Quickly, I withdrew my feet from the coolness. As I did, I felt refreshed. A deep breath came easily as I gazed again at the waters that mirrored the amber depths of the lake.

It wasn't long before children in brightly colored swimsuits burst from a caravan of cars. Mothers laden with toys, inner tubes, and towels hurried after them. With sheer delight the children ran to the lake and stopped abruptly when their tiny toes touched the snow-chilled water. They giggled, swirled the water with their feet, and then proceeded enthusiastically, without regard for the icy temperature. Grating sounds surrounded me as other children dug their shovels into the stony bank and emptied the contents into buckets that stood lopsided on the rocks. Silence lingered only between the children's intermittent screeching.

    Sharing these moments turned my sorrow into joyous memories and filled my emptiness with new life. God had given me a starting point to replenish my soul. I lingered briefly in that beautiful spot, and then went on to seek more memories to melt away the sadness.

A Reason to Dream

Chapter 1: Life's Timing

It took about two hours to get to my daughter's in Tucson, Arizona, from the mountains. My hours by the water left me in a calm state, almost a blissful stupor. However, the sharp curves around the deserted mountain road and the sun flickering off the hood held me in reality. A roadrunner attempted to keep pace with the car before darting into the desert brush. Steep hills suddenly popped into view, and just as quickly the road dipped, curved, and dipped again. It was as though I were on a roller coaster, being twisted and turned to its will. For three years my life had felt that way, but the events of December 28, 1998 catapulted me into a different reality.

In the morning I had been thinking about the chores for the day as I showered and dressed. It wasn't a particularly unusual day. My Christmas decorations were still in place. Pine boughs entwined with multi-colored lights drooped over the fruitwood china cabinet. The manger sat in the center of our small Christmas village on the living room windowsill. I gazed at the silk Christmas tree, tall and slender, that hugged the corner by the window. A freshly cut evergreen, nothing artificial, had been tradition while my children were small; a distinguished tree with pliable limbs and firm needles filled the home with the aroma of pine. It was fitting that upon seeing my imitation my son called it, "the stick." With great care I had adorned my stick with strings of popcorn, candy canes and homemade ornaments. I loved Christmas. The

3

music warmed my spirit. The excitement of people hurrying to get their special something for their special someone filled me with an abundance of energy.

The phone rang as I hummed Christmas carols and straightened the living room. David, my husband, was outside tending to some chores.

I recognized Doctor Helmon's voice immediately. We had spent many hours with him the last six months at the Cleveland Clinic. The anticipation of what he might say caused my heart to skip beats.

"I'm sorry to have to tell you this," he said calmly. "But I'm pretty sure your husband has a rare form of Lou Gehrig's disease (ALS). It's called progressive bulbar palsy. Being a nurse, I'm certain you understand this disease is terminal. I'm sorry, but there is nothing we can do, other than try to keep him comfortable."

I stood in silence, not wanting to listen. I didn't want it to be true. These wretched words, cruel and destructive, instantly drained my strength. A nauseous sensation filled the weakness that quickly spread to every fiber of my body. David was going to die.

I composed myself enough to ask, "What should I tell David?"

"Oh, don't worry about it," he said. "I'll send him a letter."

In a flash the image of a former patient— totally helpless, with a twisted body—sprang into my head. The phone slipped from my hand, hit the floor and bounced up and down like a yo-yo on a

4

string. Jolted by the noise, I watched as it spun one way and then the other. By the time I came back to my senses and grabbed the phone, all I heard was the dial tone.

All of a sudden awareness fled. I found myself standing at the kitchen sink, splashing cold water on my face. *I can't start to cry. I'll never stop. I need to be strong, especially now, for David.*

I grabbed the kitchen towel hanging on the stove handle and began to rub my face as hard as I could. My stomach twisted into a sickening knot. I wanted to vomit. Frantic, I took a couple of deep breaths to steady myself. *Where did I put the brochure I picked up at the doctor's office on Lou Gehrig? Think!*

I glanced at the desk behind me. *It must be in there.* I pulled out one drawer after another, rummaging through papers in search of the pamphlet. At last my search was fruitful. I scanned its contents in hopes of finding some answers. I didn't want David to read about this in a letter, but no words formed as I stared at the paper. Only pieces of meaningless black lines covered the page.

With all the strength I could summon, I attempted to refocus. Emotions gradually gave way to minimal logic. *Pull yourself together. Nurses have to deal with death all the time. Try to focus on the nursing process, and not on David. Otherwise, you'll be useless to him. It's been months since I've read this brochure. I don't remember if it was well-written or not. I'll have to trust that I never would have kept it, if it hadn't been.* Somehow this lifeless narrow pamphlet would have the mammoth task of telling David he was dying. In silence I stared at its rectangular size, bold print and colorful pages. The complexity of the disease seemed to be mocked by its simplicity. Without question, this task was mine, and mine alone.

As I held the brochure in my trembling hand, a painful smile crossed my lips. I thought of David with his little tuft of gray hair right in the center of his almost bald head. It was ten years since we met at a single's dance. The first time he held my hand, his touch—strong—yet tender, had swiftly sent a glow to my heart. He smiled. In an instant I had fallen in love. We married a year later.

"Who was on the phone, Baby Cakes?" David asked as he walked into the living room.

Startled I looked at the phone and then back at him, not knowing what to say. I wanted to lie. I wanted to say I didn't know or that it was a telemarketer, but I couldn't lie. He deserved better than that. It was an unavoidable task. I'd have to tell him, sooner or later.

"Did you hear me?"

"Oh! I guess I was preoccupied," I stuttered. Standing before him, I wondered if my demeanor revealed my pain. "It was Doctor Helmon. You know. . . the doctor from the Cleveland Clinic?"

David threw his work gloves on the television, "I suppose they want me to come back for more tests. Well . . just forget it. They've got all the blood and guts they're going to get out of this guy."

"No, honey. That's not what he called for." I looked down at the brochure in my hand. I took a deep breath in an attempt to control the tremor in my voice. "He called to say he thinks you have progressive bulbar palsy."

David's eyes captured mine, "What's that?"

"It's a rare form of Lou Gehrig's disease," I whispered.

I sensed I should run to him, embrace him, but feared such a move would signal my hopelessness. I stayed paralyzed.

David said nothing. Silence stayed close for an eternity. My husband, the man I loved, stood staring at me as if I could make it better, like I could make it go away.

Being the second youngest at the time his father left the family, David understood hardship. With no one to provide even the most basic essentials, he and his twelve brothers and sisters worked together to milk the cows, to plant and weed the fields, and to harvest the crops. Yet these things did not prepare him for this dreadful diagnosis. This was a hardship far beyond what either of us could comprehend.

Both shattered, we stayed separate in a hollow lapse of time. I glanced at the brochure as I tried to see through my tears.

My voice wavered as I spoke. "When we were at the neurologist's office, I picked up a brochure I think will be helpful in explaining the diagnosis. Would you like me to go over it with you?"

7

"No . . . Lou Gehrig's doesn't need much explanation. I'll read it and let you know what I think."

I heard myself say, "Sometimes people live a long time with these neurological diseases."

It was a statement that encouraged hope, a lame attempt to ease the fear. Yet in my heart I knew no hope existed. My eyes betrayed my pain as I handed David the brochure. Streams of tears spoke the truth hidden in those empty words.

Chapter 2: Discovery

The January winds blew bitterly that year. The dampness cut right to the bones of my shivers. Usually by the end of November, we were settled in Arizona or Florida for the winter with our thirty-seven foot fifth wheel. That wasn't going to happen this year. Awaiting answers for David the vehicle had been stored on some farmland, gathering snow around its skirt.

The dreariness of the month accentuated the words on the letter David held in his hand. Two short paragraphs stated the diagnosis, each with a couple of sentences. There weren't any answers to our questions. Only words like, "We are sorry to inform you…" covered the page.

Irritated by the letter David shouted, "I'm not swallowing everything they hand out. They don't have one shred of evidence to support such a thing. All my tests were negative. The first neurologist never mentioned anything like this palsy. Helmon can take his gut feelings and sell them elsewhere because this guy ain't buying."

Until the day the letter arrived, I never thought about the brochure I had given David. It had disappeared without any discussion. I assumed the letter would have the same fate. Strange, a few words on a piece of paper, and our lives changed forever. Our daily routine remained the same, but doubt lurked in the shadows of our hearts. How could we be sure of the diagnosis? Even the doctor had hesitated.

At the end of the month, we received a letter from Billy, David's brother-in-law. He was going to be in McAllen, Texas for a month and wondered if David would like to join him.

The idea excited David, "I know I'll feel better if I can get into a warmer climate. You don't mind if I go, do you?"

Since the doctor's call, things were different. His attitude lacked luster. Nothing jarred him away from the television, not even the anticipation of getting the mail.

Living with limitations would not sit well with David. The years of climbing poles and dragging heavy cables as a master electrician, had kept his lean one hundred and seventy-five pounds, strong and agile. When the first neurologist tested David's strength, the doctor grasped David's hand and told him to resist. David met the challenge with a grin and pulled the surprised doctor out of his chair.

I remember how he used to dance down the street in front of me before we were married, like a peacock showing off his feathers. When he held me in his arms while we danced, his commands were firm and smooth. It felt so good; I'd fall in love all over again.

It was a long drive, but he was mobile and still pretty strong. What could it hurt? The trip could be a diversion, perhaps capture some good times for him.

When I first heard about Lou Gehrig's disease (ALS) in a nursing class, the textbook description astounded me. Wanting to escape such a reality, fear buried the thought in the blackened depths of my mind. With this diagnosis the horror resurfaced to haunt my nights. I had transferred the images in my textbook to David, and they wouldn't stay away. I had to know the differences between the two diseases to calm my thoughts.

Since David's first neurologist promised us the details, I called his office. Upon reaching the doctor's nurse, she said I'd have to pay for an appointment to get information. I told her we had been promised an explanation. It didn't matter; it would cost $100.00 or no help.

"How can you people treat a dying man's family like this?" I shouted. "We were told as soon as we got a diagnosis your office would answer our questions. You promise information and then hang a price tag on it? Is there anything else you'd like to do to make coping more difficult?"

I didn't wait for a response. I slammed the phone into its cradle. I would do the research myself.

The day I set out for the medical library was a brisk morning, the kind that freezes the little hairs in your nose when you dare to inhale. Traffic had been light and the streets clear, so I arrived a few minutes earlier than expected. After parking the car, it was a short walk to the front door of the library. I pulled on the door's handle. Getting resistance, I noticed the deadbolt snug in its lock. I glanced at my watch. It would be another five minutes before the doors opened. I began pacing back and forth, mentally reviewing a list of journals I could examine, like the medical dictionaries and

the "Journal of the American Medical Association"
(JAMA). As I walked I raised my hands to my face,
blowing into my mittens. The tight weave along
with the double pair prevented any warmth from
getting through to ease my discomfort. Then the
deadbolt tumbled in the lock. It was nine o'clock.
The librarian stepped aside and invited me in.

The library was small in comparison to the
knowledge on display. Walls of books had been
placed on walnut shelves, scattered haphazardly
around the room. Hopefully, I'd be able to gather
the research in a brief period. However, the task
proved to be much more than I had anticipated.
Before long, the desktop was stacked with medical
books, medical dictionaries, and numerous journals.
The librarian, seeing she had buried me in books,
joined my efforts. In vain she reviewed the indexes.
The literature consistently alluded to ALS. There
was nothing on progressive bulbar palsy. As I got
ready to leave, the librarian suggested I call "Ask-
A-Nurse." I smiled politely and thanked her for the
number she wrote on a scrap of paper. I had just
completed an exhaustive search of the literature; it
didn't seem possible anyone could tell me anything
about the disease. By the same token, I had nothing
to lose.

After I arrived home, I hung my jacket in the
closet, picked up the phone and dialed the number
for "Ask-A-Nurse." Pushing the buttons for the
usual set of commands, I got to the nurse.

"I am calling to get some information on
progressive bulbar palsy."

"Thank you. I'm going to put you on hold while I find the data."

The wait seemed endless. Yet, by the time I heard her voice only a minute had passed. As the nurse began to read, her voice seemed to fade. It was as though she had moved away from the phone. I struggled to grasp her words as they passed through my mind like a hurricane, leaving the debris of a harsh reality.

I'm a professional. I shouldn't have to ask her to repeat.

My choices were clear. I could either ask or hang up without knowing about the disease. Embarrassed, I asked her to repeat the description. This time key words stood out: suffocation, paralysis, stomach tube, inability to swallow, loss of speech. The words ripped at my heart, my chest tightened.

Trembling, I asked, "Could you please mail a copy to me?"

"I'm very sorry, but due to the copyright laws I'm not permitted to do that. I do happen to know Muscular Dystrophy (MDA) sponsors a support group for ALS. They will be having their monthly meeting tonight at seven at the Episcopal Church. Why don't you try to make the meeting? You'll be able to find out more, at least what type of help is available."

Slowly, I replaced the phone in its cradle. Tears spilled from my eyes as uncontrollable sobs captured my being. Deep inside, my shrouded denial had been exposed.

Carolee O'Neill

How will I be able to take care of David, the household and my business, all alone?

As the sun had dipped below the horizon, I needed to decide whether to go to the meeting. The thought of doing one more thing that day seemed impossible. My body ached as I got up. I needed rest more than a meeting. In spite of how I felt, I could not excuse myself. I had to learn as much as possible before David came home and this was my chance. Perhaps a nice meal and a shower would help. An hour and a half later, I arrived at the church.

The sign on the church door gave directions to the meeting. Following them led me to a typical church basement finished with eight foot ceilings and massive space that could be divided into additional rooms. Everything felt cold: the tables, the chairs and the floor. I began to shiver. I folded my arms under my midriff to contain body heat as the moderator stood up. I listened intently as she opened the meeting, introducing individuals and their caregivers. Good humor filled the room as different individuals gave accounts of their lives the last month. I sat in silence while my ears hummed a monotone. Reality told me I belonged in this group even if my emotions were in denial. Regardless, nothing could have prepared me for a room full of people with blatant diseases, not even my nurses' training. Too soon it was my turn. My mouth was dry, words stuck in my throat, faces turned toward me with saddened eyes. They waited with patience as I struggled to compose myself. Individuals encouraged me to say whatever was in my heart.

Someone said it was OK to cry. Gradually, I
relinquished my burden into the care of people who
knew what it meant to live moment to moment.
Something I would have to learn to do.

Chapter 3: Options

Any communication with David while he was in Texas was rare. He had limited access to a phone and no computer for email. On the occasions he did call, he avoided talking about how he felt, but a wife knows. Joy was missing from his voice. Jokes weren't funny. He sounded so tired.

By March Billy would be leaving McAllen, Texas, in spite of the unpredictable weather in the northern part of the country. David would have to follow. In David's condition, the temperature change would be hard for him to bear.

Concerned about David, Billy told him about a naturopathic physician in San Antonio, Texas.

David called, excited about the news. "It's worth a try. What have I got to lose? Maybe the doc can find out what is really wrong with me."

Sadness filled my heart, but I knew he needed to explore every avenue, even if I believed the diagnosis. The similarities of the disease with the symptoms were too convincing: more difficulty swallowing and more slurred speech. It didn't matter; I agreed.

David kept the appointment with the doctor, but no diagnosis was made. More blood work and body scans were completed. In exchange for the legal tender, David was overwhelmed with lists of instructions and bags of remedies. The money was flying out of the door faster than it was coming in. Without a doubt, David remained positive—the naturopathic physician would cure him.

Diligently, he hung his routine on the side of our refrigerator after he got home. Bottles of all types were lined up like little soldiers on the bottom shelf of the kitchen cabinet: small round black pills, assorted capsules, tiny powdery tablets and pellets that came in little paper sacks. They filled his hand between meals and before and after he ate. As swallowing became more difficult, he used a food processor to mash or grind his food. He stayed faithful to his routine even though he was a meat and potatoes guy. Gradually, he excluded supplements, until he only used the ones that dissolved easily in his mouth.

Chapter 4: Doctor's Orders

A couple of months after David returned
from Texas, we were sent to Doctor Weiss by the
Muscular Dystrophy Association (MDA). He was a
neurologist whose practice was a reasonable drive
from our home. It seemed like a miracle that there
was someone close who specialized in this rare
disease. After interviewing David, Doctor Weiss
became his primary physician for the progressive
bulbar palsy.

A month later the dark-haired, heavyset
doctor told David he needed a stomach tube. As he
spoke, he continued to write at his desk, never
looking into our eyes.

"If you don't do this, the chore of chewing
your food will consume all of your calories. You
need those calories to nourish your body, not to
chew your food," he scolded. "You've already
begun to lose too much weight."

With his display of attitude and body
language, the good doctor hadn't won any brownie
points with David. Instead, David argued, bound to
his independence. With the determination of a mule
he pushed off the surgery.

In the meantime another option surfaced.
Our chiropractor wanted to try a diagnostic tool
called "Contact Reflex Analysis." Again David was
sure the treatment would save his life. In spite of
David's diligence with the additional supplements
from the chiropractor, he continued to grow weaker,
and eating became more of a job than a joy.

As other difficulties forced him to make decisions he did not want to make, he expressed his anger with profanities. I held my words. I knew David, the man coping with the disease, loved his God. He knew God's Word and had served Him faithfully as a teacher, an usher, and a choir member.

By the spring of 2000, a month later, David agreed to the surgery. This brought a flood of professionals into our lives. While we were in the hospital, a nurse discussed wound care, social services told us what services were available and respiratory therapy coached David on the use of his oxygen, all within minutes of each other. I wondered how a layperson would be able to cope with all of it. The medical jargon rattled off at record speed and the list of available services would be overwhelming, not to mention what each service had to offer. Then there was the unfamiliar equipment from departments, like respiratory therapy and physical therapy.

Armed with the information, I took David home. So far there weren't any surprises, but that soon changed. Later that evening I couldn't control David's pain. I called the emergency department where we were supposed to go the next morning. But no matter how pleasant or how cantankerous I got, the nurse stuck to her agenda. We had an appointment in the morning at nine o'clock, it could wait until then. To say this was upsetting would be to downplay my newly acquired vocabulary. All I could do to ease his pain was apply wrapped packets of ice.

After suffering all night from a procedure that was supposed to be simple, I insisted he be medicated as soon as we arrived at the emergency room.

"We have to wait until the doctor comes," a stocky little nurse said. "We don't have orders, so we can't administer any medication."

"You don't have standing orders for your surgical patient?" *I can't believe this.*

"The doctor was supposed to be here thirty minutes ago. So David is just supposed to lie there and suffer, right?"

"Sorry, but there's nothing we can do until the doctor gets here."

Another half hour passed. I paced from David's gurney to the hallway, hoping I'd see the doctor coming. When he finally showed up, he walked briskly over to David and began pushing around the surgical site. David screamed. The doctor continued to push.

Shocked, I whispered in amazement, "What are you doing?"

"I don't understand why he's in so much pain. The area isn't rigid; in fact it's soft."

Patience gone, I snapped, "He hasn't been adequately medicated, that's why. He needs to have something, now!"

The doctor turned to see who was giving him orders, "I'm his wife and I'm also an RN. I tried to reach you last night so this wouldn't happen, but I was told I'd have to wait until morning. This is ridiculous. David shouldn't have to suffer like this. I would appreciate it if you'd write an order so something can be administered right away."

"Excuse me, ma'am, I'm the dietitian and I'm here to show you how to do a tube feeding."

David's face twisted in pain as he rolled back and forth with his arms clasped around his stomach. I glanced quickly from David to the dietitian, then back again. Trying to watch the doctor and comfort David, I turned to the dietitian. "This isn't a good time. You'll have to come back later."

"I can't, ma'am. I have a full schedule."

He began the instructions, talking at the same time as the doctor. Understanding became impossible with my hearing loss.

What is he, dense or something? Can't he see I'm too busy to listen to him?

The doctor turned, looking at me like the god he thought he was, and began to walk out of the room, "I've ordered some Demerol. I'll tell the nurse to bring it in."

"Wait a minute!" I insisted. "I have some questions."

He kept his pace. Angrily, I pursued with the dietitian right on my heels, his rhetoric never missing a beat. Being intent on getting the medication for David, I had to go back and wait in David's cubicle. Wearily, I continued to pace between the doorway and David as the dietitian followed. Not able to grasp his words, I tried to ignore him. Five minutes, then ten minutes went by. *That's it!* I went to the nurse's station, with the dietitian in pursuit.

21

"Ma'am, you're not going to know how to do this procedure if you don't listen."

"I'll take my chances. I told you this wasn't a good time, but you insisted on continuing."

Arriving at the nursing station, I found nurses standing around in jovial conversation.

Angered by the scene, I demanded, "Who's supposed to be handling David's care? He was supposed to be medicated and it hasn't happened."

A nurse staring at a monitor said, "Oh, we're about to take him to the floor. They'll give him a shot when he gets there."

Struggling to maintain my composure, I said, "You mean you intend to transfer this patient without medicating him?"

"Well…he'll get something as soon as he gets to the floor."

"I know how floor transfers work. He'll be sitting up there for another hour before the nurse has time to read his chart. That's not going to happen. I suggest you check his chart and administer the Demerol the doctor ordered, now! Otherwise, I'm going to your supervisor. I'll expect you to be in his room within the next five minutes."

In less than three minutes a young nurse entered with a syringe, wiped the IV port with alcohol and emptied the syringe in record time. I stood horrified as I watched a red streak follow the medication up David's arm.

"What's the matter with you? You administered the medication too fast and have irritated his vein. Send the head nurse in."

A Reason to Dream

The head nurse apologized as she checked David's arm. She said she would complete an incident report. David was finally resting comfortably. I went to the restroom after the transfer and cried until I thought I would vomit.

The complications from the surgery caused David to stay in the hospital for two more days. The readmission triggered another chain reaction. Just before he was released, the social worker came again and suggested we be interviewed by Home Health Care. Their personnel came the day after I took David home. We were asked myriads of questions and signed lots of papers, not knowing if our explanations were complete. By the time they finished the interview, the nurse suggested David be referred to Hospice.

"I'll call the hospice in the county where your doctor practices," the nurse said. "They can call you for an appointment."

"I don't understand. Why can't we use the one in Saint Joe county?"

"That's the way the system is set up. All I know is you're supposed to use the hospice in the same county where your doctor practices."

The next day we went through the same interview with hospice—more paperwork, same questions. However, our questions would be answered at a later date. They assumed I would be his caregiver. Within a couple of days, we were told David had been accepted as a patient. Joyce would be the assigned nurse.

Days passed. We were consumed by the hospice routines, spaced feedings, dressing changes,

23

administration of medications and activities of daily living. I had joined David in his ritual of pills and remedies, even though he continued to fail. I was doing everything possible to keep a dying man alive.

*   *   *

The comings and goings of hospice and other medical personnel left us with very little privacy. Everyday our home filled with more medical equipment; extra oxygen tanks occupied the closet off the hallway along with a walker that David refused to use. The spare bedroom took on its own harsh reality of illness. The overnight table, enslaved with tubing from the CPap breathing machine, kept David's airway open while he slept. The harness for the face attached to the oxygen cup to cover David's nose and mouth, leaving proof of its past presence. From morning to night, the suction machine moved from the living room to the bedroom on top of the utility cart, leaving a path on the already well-worn carpet. During the day, the machine sat next to David's recliner where it performed its on—off routine. Hours of war stories and documentaries blared from the television, interrupted only by the sucking sound of the machine.

As the disease progressed, indistinguishable words slipped from David's mouth. Not willing to recognize another loss, he refused to use the pads of paper placed around the home to write his words. I would run back and forth between David and my chores in an attempt to understand him. The combination of my inability to understand and his inability to speak—well, tempers were more than short. David's denial walked hand-in-hand with my exasperation.

After several months of this, I began to ignore his attempt to speak. Fatigue had won the power struggle. David didn't give up. The contest, one I hadn't wanted to enter, continued for another month. Then one day without warning, he picked up a pencil and began to write. I never said a word. He had surrendered his thoughts to paper after an honorable battle. At first he wrote only a word or two. As he became more comfortable with writing, the words began to flow. He wrote volumes, like a kid with a new toy. In a small way, socialization had been reborn. Although the new media didn't award fewer steps, the steps taken were not out of frustration.

Chapter 5: Jobs

Almost six months had passed since David received his diagnosis. We had adjusted to the routine as much as possible, but now we had to figure out what to do with the Mountain Aire fifth wheel. We considered selling it because the monthly mortgage payment put an unnecessary strain on our finances. In the past, with David's permission of course, I towed the twenty-six foot fifth wheel several times. It was just my size. I loved the feeling. I'd make-believe the highway led to a secret place hidden to everyone but me. However, our thirty-eight foot Mountain Aire was a different story. I only towed it once, and that was enough.

Every year around the first of August, David's extended family in Pennsylvania had a reunion. In preparation for the event, David put hours into his new toy as he washed, waxed and loaded it for show and tell. Heading east, he sat proudly behind the wheel of our tow truck until just before he turned onto the freeway. Then he jumped out of the driver's seat, and he told me I should drive for a few miles. *What? My husband is actually going to let me drive?* Yes, he wanted me to do just that; I should share in his grandiose feeling of towing the Mountain Aire. I'll never know why. When I pulled the smaller unit, he'd brace himself with one hand on the dash and the other on the door.

Everything was going fine the first few miles. There didn't seem to be any difference, as far as I could see. So I relaxed. Cruising at an easy fifty-five miles an hour on a sunny day, I felt a tug on the truck. I glanced to my left and saw that the fifth wheel had begun to jackknife, taking an enormous sway to the left as the truck swayed to the right. The grandiose feeling left. David panicked. I wanted to join him, but I didn't have time. For some reason I did exactly what anyone in the state of panic would do. I took my foot off the gas. For the next few minutes the camper glided back and forth, until it finally settled down behind the truck. Frankly, it would've suited me just fine if David would've been behind the wheel when we learned that we needed a bigger truck to handle this monstrosity. With that little incident, I preferred to stay out of the driver's seat. Even if all had gone well with the unit, I wouldn't have been able to hook up the heavy-duty Reese hitch.

As everything wasn't copasetic, the logical solution was to turn it over to a dealership.

After contacting several dealerships, I connected with a fellow in Richmond, Indiana.

"I'd be thrilled to have the unit on the lot," Ralph said. "We don't have anything like it, so it would be an asset, a great leader."

Believing the salesman's sincerity, David hooked up the Mountain Aire to the truck for the last time. His pad lay on the ground next to his tools. He worked in silence, never revealing his feelings. Concerned that the trip would be too much for him, I suggested we ask someone to go along. He insisted he'd be OK. In his weakened condition, hooking up a fifth wheel and towing it one hundred and eighty miles seemed like an insurmountable

27

task. Even taking a shower and getting dressed had become a chore.

"I'll be fine," David wrote on his pad. "I wouldn't feel safe with somebody else towing it. All they'd be doing is asking questions I couldn't answer. It's my job, and I need to take care of it."

All I could do was my job—follow with the car.

It was a bittersweet trip to Richmond. The Mountain Aire brought back memories as I followed David. A curio, a place for keepsakes, a small tree, and the crib at Christmas, separated the dining room and the living room. We had replaced the lime-green recliner with a Roland electronic piano. Just as David had no intention of living in our twenty-six foot fifth wheel for six months, I had no intention of traveling without an instrument.

The sun flashed off the top of the coach, reminding me of the first time David washed and waxed the camper. I had to chuckle. I wasn't allowed to help. I couldn't make the circles right with the wax, I guessed.

By the time he was halfway through the job, he grumbled, "This is like washing and waxing an elephant."

Not long after that he gave me a section to do. I believe its size, if nothing else, had caused him to reconsider. I promised I would rub as hard as I could and with not very big circles. Up the ladder I went to fulfill my mission. After a few moments I came across an indentation about three or four feet from the top of the unit. Perplexed, I asked David what had happened.

He looked at the spot and shrugged. "Aw…it must be from one of those truck mirrors."

Almost falling off the ladder, I gasped, "You mean the ones attached to the semis'?"

A scowl crossed his face as he looked up at me. I was demoted to the hubcaps.

After miles of looking at the back of the fifth wheel, precious memories were replaced with the thoughts of our future. I didn't want to fall into despair and doing so wouldn't change a thing. I needed to find something positive to occupy my mind. I turned on the radio to see if I could locate some soothing music, but there was only hard rock and country western. With the latter I couldn't understand the lyrics. The hard rock—well, my hearing aids turned that into noise.

Traveling in the car as a child with my older five siblings was an unforgettable experience. Being the youngest, my opinion on how we'd pass the time did not carry much weight. Sooner or later somebody, usually my older sister, would suggest we play fruit and vegetable games or sing songs. This did wonders for our parents' sanity. It kept us from fighting and asking our dad if we were there yet, fifty thousand times. One of our favorite songs was "Tell Me Why." The family divided into sopranos, basses, altos, and tenors. Perfect harmony, so we thought, filled the car. Even Mom and Dad joined in. David didn't like to sing or talk when he drove. He just stared straight ahead. I often wondered what he was thinking during all those cross-country miles.

Carolee O'Neill

Following David now, the melodies played
on my emotional strings until I found myself
humming. It felt comforting and relaxing. The urge
of song burst from within. I had to sing all three
stanzas of "Tell Me Why." Continuing on I sang,
"You Are My Sunshine," "Oh what a Beautiful
Morning," "Zip-Da-Dee-Do-Dah" *and* "Mares Eat
Oats." The future had been blocked temporarily. I
drove with a light heart.

    After my concert I basked in delight. Then a
melody sounded in my head, a soothing, graceful
melody with lyrics so meaningful tears filled my
eyes. Fearful that the tune would escape, I sang it
over and over again. Even at that the melody began
to slip, a different tone here, a different lyric there.
In the past I had chastised myself for not writing
down a lovely sonnet before it vanished forever. I
had to get this one on paper. My right hand
rummaged through my purse for something,
anything would do. I found an old grocery list that
was blank on the one side. I centered the paper on
the pad that housed the horn, focusing my eyes
partly on traffic and partly on writing. I maneuvered
the steering wheel with my knees and a tight grip
with my left hand. The lyrics rode up and down on
the tiny indentation of the horn's leather pad. A
foolish act, I told myself, but I continued to draw
the staff, placing each note on its proper line or
space.

    *If David saw me I'd be smashed potatoes.
But then I could always remind him about the truck
mirrors.*

I wasn't about to let this melody escape into nothingness.

I will always remember the dreams that
were promised, the dreams that were all left behind.
Yes, I'll always remember the dreams we
discovered and the gifts that they were to my soul…

After we returned home I played it for David, never telling him how it had been composed. He loved music, so much so I'd sometimes find him sitting on the floor outside of the music room, listening to me play. When I'd catch him, he'd grin sheepishly like a little boy.

Before I realized it we had arrived at the dealership. Once again music fulfilled its purpose. It had gotten me through the silence one experiences while waiting for time to pass. Things moved rather quickly from that point on. We found the salesman who promised to sell the truck and the fifth wheel and signed the necessary papers. He said used campers were plentiful, so he couldn't guarantee a quick sale.

The task completed, David climbed into the passenger's seat of our 1990 Dodge Spirit. On the way home, we didn't share thoughts about the sale of the camper. It seemed like it was still ours. It was just in another place. A month later reality snapped us out of denial when both the truck and the camper sold. Our freedom to travel was gone.

Chapter 6: The Simple Things

The summer of 2000 would hopefully bring David's family for a visit. With an uncertain future, countless decisions needed to be made. Being married only eight years, I felt these decisions belonged to his family, not me. Decisions like who he wanted to have the power tools and electrical equipment in the garage? In the basement, dust-ridden boxes were stashed on the top shelf in the laundry room. They were filled with power plugs and computer parts entangled in their own cords. Personal papers from his army days sat next to the computer parts in a partially opened box, along with unpublished poetry. His poetry showed his heart and often his sense of humor, but mostly his love for our Father.

A SONG OF PRAISE

I work and worry, stew and fret
On most days I just forget
All the beauty there is to see
All that my Lord has given to me

I've felt the touch of a loving hand
the look that says I understand
I've seen the joy of a child at play
Shared their tears and laughter gay

I've been caressed by a gentle breeze
that comes ashore from off the seas
I've felt the softness of a winter snow
And the warmth of a fireplace, all aglow

A Reason to Dream

I've watched the billowy clouds roll by
to bask in sunlight from on high
I've seen the mighty rivers wide
the oceans ebb and their flowing tides

I've played upon the silvery sand
and on the mountain top did stand
I've seen the beauty of each living tree
from its tiny seed to its majesty

Lord! What I see leaves me amazed
I shall daily sing thy praise
With all thy power and mighty deeds
My Lord, you still would walk with me
                    David Joseph B.
                    1933 - 2001

What to do with these things was the easy part. The tough decisions came when the minister suggested David put his papers in order and make his final arrangements. David agreed, but as soon as the minister left he would change his mind.

A few days later David would change his mind again. Trying to accommodate his wishes, I called a mortician who was recommended by a friend. The appointment was set for the next morning at ten o'clock. When the doorbell rang, I opened it to find a gaunt, pale fellow dressed in a black suit and a crisp white shirt. His eyes eluded mine. This was not going to work. Out of courtesy I invited him in. David's jaw dropped. I swear his eyes reflected the grim reaper dragging a dead body off the street after a gun fight. David returned to his job of suctioning; the machine's routine changed to "on." When the grim reaper didn't take the hint, David flipped from one channel to another on the television. Several uncomfortable moments passed as I attempted to gather information. Realizing David was not going to acknowledge the man's presence, I went to the door, thanked him for stopping and ushered him out.

It was a week before I got another request. This time I called a friend who was a mortician. Daniel, a lanky fellow, arrived meticulously dressed in a business suit, shook David's hand and proceeded to direct all of the conversation toward me. I continued to look toward David, hoping he would get the hint and include him in the conversation. Unfortunately, that didn't work. It didn't take an Einstein to see David wasn't going to sign on the dotted line with Daniel, either.

In bold print, David wrote, "FORGET IT." I began to wonder if we'd ever get anything settled before we ran out of morticians.

With another visit from the minister, we were back on the merry-go-around. The routine repeated itself with David agreeing, and then changing his mind. Embarrassed and frustrated, I approached him as gently as I could.

"Honey, there are so many things I don't know, like which children you'd want to have certain things."

Grabbing his pad he scribbled in big print, "YOU JUST CAN'T WAIT TO GET RID OF ME, CAN YOU? CALL THE HOMELESS

SHELTER. I'LL GO DOWN THERE AND LIVE.
YOU JUST WANT ME TO DIE. WELL, I'M NOT
DEAD YET."

Angered by his attack, I shouted, "That's it,
Buster! Nobody knows when they're going to die.
And the way things are going around here, I'll be
gone long before you are. So knock it off! I'm not
treating you like you're sick any longer. That gravy
train has just ended. I'm going to treat you like my
husband, and if you don't like it, tough! If you tick
me off, I'm going to holler at you. And if I tick you
off, you can holler at me. I'm all through walking
on egg shells. If you think it's so darn much fun
trying to make final arrangements for someone you
love, go and make mine and see how much fun it is.
We will live the best we can from day to day or
from minute to minute, if we have to. That's the
way it's going to be. Understand?"

David stared at me wide-eyed. Then he
nodded.

I lay awake after retiring, wondering about
what David had written on his pad. I felt crushed by
his attack, unappreciated. I didn't want him dead. I
understood he needed his independence. I accepted
his mood swings, his decisions in refusing
equipment, like a walker or a portable suction
machine, even though I knew his choices
jeopardized his care. After what he wrote, it was
clear he thought I wanted him dead as soon as
possible. I had gotten caught up in my nursing role
and what others thought I should be doing. David
had responded with acting out behavior, like
throwing the remote across the room or breaking

35

something of mine. It was another night like many others. I fell asleep praying for courage and the understanding necessary to hear what David actually meant.

The days became easier after these feelings were vented. We were able to make some decisions, review our documents and update our wills. Once again I had become David's wife, not just his nurse. David was once again my husband, rubbing my feet at night the best he could, sharing in decision making, cracking jokes and hollering at me in big print on his tablet.

Chapter 7: Independence

Days melted into months, pushed forward by chores. Many times I wondered why I bothered to make the bed in the morning. It seemed like I had barely gotten up and it was time to go to bed. Hospice provided an aide, but she was limited to activities of daily living. Being a very private person, David wasn't about to allow anyone to see him nude or watch while he went to the bathroom. By the time I prepared everything for the aide's visit, I could have done the jobs myself, without losing our privacy. So the visits, three times a week, became more of a hassle than a help.

Like everything else, there were trade-offs. One of the aides gave us a one eight hundred number so we wouldn't have to make long distance calls to get the nurse. The number went to the hospital switchboard. All we had to do was ask to be transferred.

The hospice nurse came every other week to take David's blood pressure, listen to his lungs and check his stomach tube. Knowing Joyce was coming made me feel a little safer. Outside of that we were on our own, enduring many hours of uncertainty.

As David became weaker my concern for his safety grew. It bothered me to leave him alone while I went to the store. Although he said he'd be fine, my nursing judgment told me it wasn't a good idea. I had heard about Lifeline through nursing several years before. It seemed a logical solution in spite of the cost. He would have help as soon as something happened, and when I went shopping I would have some peace of mind.

I discussed the telephone system with David and explained how it worked. "All you'll have to do is wear the Lifeline around your neck or on your belt."

He didn't object, so I assumed he agreed. A week later, I watched dumbfounded as he pulled the two thousand dollar unit out of its connections, walked to the middle of the room, and dropped it from five feet off the ground. Sickened, I stared as it plunged downward, wondering how I would pay for a broken unit. What would I tell the people at Lifeline—my husband deliberately broke it?

As it hit the carpet, I cried out in anger, "It better not be broken or the money will come out of your hide!"

He sneered, wiped the sputum from his mouth with a tissue, and walked back to his chair.

I knelt on the carpet and took the unit in my hands. I turned it over, looking for cracks or broken pieces. I found none. I told myself it was the disease. My David could never be that cynical. Carrying the unit back to the desk, I plugged the phone line into the wall, praying I would get a dial tone. I put the receiver to my head. The tone sounded. I sighed, thankfully.

In a rage I turned to David, "That wasn't funny! What in the world is wrong with you?"

He grabbed his pad and wrote, "I'm not wearing that thing and I'm not using that phone."

"Why didn't you tell me that before I went to all the trouble of getting it for you? If you don't use it, we'll be paying for it anyway. It's up to you! But I'll tell you this much, mister. It's staying, whether you like it or not. You'll just have to get used to it."

I knew as his condition worsened, we'd both feel less safe. As with other things that he rejected, he'd later accept it. I could only hold to that possibility.

Chapter 8: Matters of Privacy

Christmas came too quickly that year. I don't remember any snow. Maybe it was there. Maybe it wasn't. There wouldn't be any company; no one would break the monotony of the daily routine. Half-heartedly I put up *my stick* and some decorations, hoping to fill the emptiness with a speck of joy. The television reflected the dim glow of the multi-colored Christmas lights as a documentary flashed across the screen. It seemed like a contradiction, war stories depicting death and commercials with carolers chanting, "Joy to the World."

Not wanting to watch war stories, I set up a card table in the lower level so I could make some homemade Christmas cards. I felt they'd add a special piece of love to a blessed holiday. It was a meticulous job, cutting out the material, printing the text and painting the hand-drawn figures with watercolors, but I loved it. They offered me an escape from reality, transforming strife to peaceful moments. Proudly, I counted them after the final touches had been applied. There were thirteen delicate cards and envelopes finished. It was just a beginning; I had many more to make. Momentarily, I paged through my new Christmas magazine for more ideas, leaving it next to the cards I had finished.

*   *   *

Early the next morning the receptionist from hospice called, saying our regular aide was ill. We loved Pattie. Her hugs were plentiful and she had a laugh that came all the way from her toes. However, today we would be getting a replacement. I didn't think much about it because Pattie did such a fabulous job. Nevertheless, I would have to familiarize the new aide with her tasks and the house.

When the replacement aide's duty ended, I went downstairs to work on more cards. Glancing at the table, I was troubled. Only fragments of my work remained. The cards and my magazine were gone. Thinking I must have put them someplace else, I searched every room, countertop, drawer and desktop, but couldn't find them.

The cards were down here this morning when I did the laundry. Then I ran to the store for a couple of things. Who had been here? Was somebody other than the aide in the house? I see she put David's dirty laundry on the washing machine, so she must've been down here. Questioning David, he wrote that no one else had been in the house. I called hospice to report the incident.

Joyce apologized that the magazine had been taken. "It was an accident. She didn't mean to take it. I'll bring it back when I come for David's next visit."

"What about the cards?"

"She said she didn't take them. With all that's been going on you probably put them someplace safe. I'm sure they'll turn up."

The cards were never recovered. My only safe space had been violated. *How can I ever trust anyone other than Pattie?*

*   *   *

Everyday shopping had become a way to hide my feelings. A plan, I found, that doesn't work at Christmas-time. The stores were jammed with people rushing to buy their perfect gifts. They were doing what had brought joy to my heart. Now it fed the emptiness with sorrow.

On Christmas Eve David wrote on his pad that he wanted to go to the evening service at church.

How does he think he can do that? He's weak and he doesn't have a portable suction machine. I wish he would've listened to me when I told him he should get one.

The thought had barely crossed my mind when I found him standing in front of me in his gray pin-striped suit. His favorite white Kleenex, cold care size, was stuffed in his mouth. A grin, partially hidden by the Kleenex, and the twinkle in his eye said how proud he was of his inventiveness. I had to laugh at the sight. As soon as I started, he started. There we stood like two little kids, sniggering about his demeanor. Shaking my head and still laughing, I grabbed my leather coat from the hall closet and asked him to wait while I warmed the car. The thought that someone might find the Kleenex uncouth, momentarily crossed my mind. It vanished as David got into the car, still grinning, and clutching his pencil and pad.

I stood close as he climbed the steps of the First United Methodist Church. Before we entered I looked at David. He was still grinning. It was show time and he was the main attraction. His dry sense of humor was one of the things I loved about him when we first met. I'm sure the anticipation of what people might think would thrill his sense of humor and provide some interesting conversation.

Entering the church, people turned in surprise. David's grin broadened. Everyone began to walk toward us, shaking our hands and welcoming us with a jovial, "Merry Christmas." With each handshake, his frail one hundred and thirty pounds swayed up and down. I hated to stop people from greeting him, but the paralysis had forced his torso and head forward, leaving him in an unstable position. My concern that he might fall quickly dissipated as I watched him reach for one hand after another until he had to sit down. His slight frame had been sustained from the energy and the caring of the congregation.

After a moment's rest he pointed at Phil, the head usher.

Surely, he doesn't think he can do that?

The next thing I knew I was escorting my grinning husband over to Phil.

David wrote on his pad, "Usher?*"*

"You want to usher?" Phil asked.

David made a mumbled aha sound, as he attempted to nod.

"Sure."

By the time David reached the last couple of pews his strength began to fail. Seeing this, Phil took over. The funny-looking wad of Kleenex stuffed in David's mouth never seemed to be visible to anyone.

43

Carolee O'Neill

Arriving home, I turned on the tree lights
and the decorative lights that adorned our home. In
their dim glow I handed David his Christmas gift.
He promptly handed one to me marked, "To My
Baby Cakes," a heartfelt surprise. He had convinced
Pattie to buy the gift, a pair of slippers. I put them
on, making a fuss over their color and perfect fit.
After David had opened his gifts, we sat in the
living room in silence, listening to Christmas music.
We sat for a long time holding each other, hoping
the moment would last forever.

A New Day
The morning sun, its face aglow
stands staring down at me.
The golden shafts dance to and fro
through branches of a tree.

Its gentle warmth so slowly dries
the drops of morning dew
and in its bright and shining rays
it sails its sky of blue.

The magic of this new born day
like no other has there been
It's that I stopped along the way
to let my Lord come in.

Like the rays of sun a shining
He dwells with us on earth
You need but pause each morning
to meet His new day's birth.
by David Joseph B.

Chapter 9: Putting It Together

The hospitals had begun their RN cutbacks in 1984. The forced retirement gave me the opportunity to explore the possibility of a business. I decided on real estate. Being successful for the first few years, I opened my own company. However, after twelve years of running the business, it became obvious that the grind of managing a fulltime business along with David's care wouldn't be possible. The handwriting was on the wall, lines on the contracts were not filled in, I was missing things—critical information, like dates. I was making too many mistakes.

A couple of years earlier, while attending a closing for a client, I had run into an attorney whom I admired.

"How have you been, Joe? I haven't seen you in awhile," I said, heartily shaking his hand.

"I've been busy shutting down my practice. With my wife ill I don't want to start making mistakes and end up going out in flames."

"Joe…you're too good for that."

"No-no, I'm not. I've seen it happen too many times. And I don't want it to happen to me."

The stage was set for my drama to play out the same way. The medical profession had already recorded several hefty diagnoses in my chart. I had ignored the signs of failing health, both physical and emotional. Running into Joe caused these truths to surface. I was no longer sure David would die before me. Following Joe's advice would be the smartest thing I could do. I began referring my clients to other agents. Later in the year 2000, I closed the doors of my business and the doors on another chapter of our lives.

A Reason to Dream

Chapter10: Not to Worry

As usual January brought a coldness that drew the moisture to its heart. The humidifier ran day and night, but with little success. Even with adequate hydration, David's secretions continued to thicken.

Joyce tried to tell David not to suction so often because it would cause more secretions. Looking into his eyes, which were once so confident and strong I saw they were now wide with fear. His upper torso weaved back and forth as he attempted to voice a *no*. Under his command the machine would run.

As one would expect, the more difficult the disease became to manage, the more horrendous thoughts plagued my mind. How well I remember the first time he choked. An automatic reflex came from my youth, and I hit him on the back. It worked, but I should have grabbed the tubing and suctioned him. Guilt reminded me that I was a nurse. I should have known better. The question remained. How would I respond the next time? What if I wouldn't be able to help him? How would I ever live with that?

Worry became my constant companion. I dreaded checking on him during the night for fear I had lost him. In the morning I'd compensate by taking my shower and dressing before going into his room. *This is the smart thing to do—then I'd be ready for anything. Even the minister said so.* This accomplished nothing except to add more guilt to my overburdened spirit.

Circumstances deprived us of companionship and socialization. We thirsted for a witty soul to knock on our door, just for the fun of it. However, time continued to fill our days with schedules, not people. On occasion a well-meaning neighbor or past acquaintance would venture into our home. After the initial hellos, they'd fiddle with a magazine or the newspaper. Their uneasiness resulted in unnatural conversation, meaningless laughter and bad jokes that were meant to lift our spirits.

Other well-meaning individuals assumed David lacked spirituality. They needed to save his soul with some spiritual poetry about Christianity or lessons written by man instead of God.

As David had been an ardent reader of the Bible, that didn't set well. Then they suggested that if David wasn't going to listen to them, I'd have to make sure he was saved. Somehow we managed to humor the individuals until I could get them out of the door. The chore of satisfying others took its toll on both of us. Weary, my spirit searched for a haven, for silence.

With little exposure to the outside world, I asked Joyce for some volunteers to share time with David. I also requested someone to stay with him while I went to church on Sunday. Hospice called and said a lady by the name of Ginny would be at our home on Sunday at ten.

The following Sunday our front doorbell rang at ten sharp. Expecting to see an elderly person, or at least someone middle-aged, I opened the door to welcome the lady. To my surprise our guest was a well-groomed, regal, young woman with a perky smile. She couldn't have been more than twenty-five. David's eyes sparkled. We were impressed.

Before I left the house, I laughed as I watched David scurry to write messages to Ginny on his pad. Then he'd hand her the pad, grinning while he waited for her to read his notes. Ginny would respond, hand the pad back and David would scribble another sentence or two. Witty conversation was taking place between them. Ginny brought lightheartedness, meaning, and life back into our home, and it was sincere.

Chapter 11: German Heartiness

It was the spring of 2001. Over the winter, we had some water damage which caused ice to back up under the shingles. The ice melted from the warmth of the house and found a pathway into the interior walls and the ceiling. The entire ceiling and front wall had to be treated and painted. Realizing this, we decided that as long as we were going to have a mess, we might as well replace the carpet and the kitchen vinyl. Having second thoughts, I approached David with what I thought would be a better idea.

"Why don't we set some money aside for the work to be done later? It will be a tremendous task to say the least, especially now."

He wrote, "No, do the work now."

"David, there will be a lot of dust and all kinds of odors from the paint and glue. It certainly will not make breathing easier. Remember, you have emphysema and asthma on top of the palsy."

He held his pad up higher as he leaned a little forward and pointed, "No, do work now."

I knew that it wouldn't be a good situation, so I went to Joyce for support. She would talk some sense into him. When she arrived for her bi-weekly visit, I took her aside and told her my concerns with the dust, the glue and the paint odors.

She went to David asking, "David does the smell of paint bother you?"

David shook his head, "no."

Angered by a question I considered stupid, I cried, "That was before he had progressive bulbar palsy, asthma and emphysema."

She giggled and David grinned.

I stomped out of the room and into my bedroom. I slammed the door as hard as I could, finding myself trapped by my own exit. I began hitting my pillow until I dropped to my knees, crying.

Not having the nurse's support, I asked David's family and friends to take him for a few days while the work was being done. They declined, saying they were afraid they wouldn't be able to manage him if something went wrong. That was understandable. It was a scary situation for a professional, much less for someone without training. Not finding help amongst family or friends, I checked other resources in the community. An elderly couple, who lived about thirty- five miles from us, took care of disabled people on a short term basis. The charges for their services were fair and the home was clean. I told David about the people. Not getting an argument, we took a drive on Sunday afternoon so he could meet them and see the home. He grunted as I drove into their driveway. He spent very little time looking at the accommodations he would have for the two weeks.

Without hesitation, he wrote on his pad, "Let's go! I'm not staying in this dumpy little place."

I wanted to shout sense into his head, but I knew I'd be wasting my energy. I'd need that for the scheduled work. I had spent two weeks moving furniture into the garage and I'd have to move it back after the work was finished.

My three boys planned to come on Memorial Day weekend to help with the work. Just before they came, David insisted that the entire first floor be screwed down after the carpet was removed, and he wanted all the walls painted and re-papered. With this addition to the schedule, the job went from big to huge.

Before the boys arrived, my friend Bob, who was also my insurance agent, offered to pull up the old vinyl in the kitchen. He said he'd be over the next day to start the job. As I needed a few things from the store, I asked David if he would be OK for about an hour. He assured me he would. I laid the Lifeline remote on his cart next to him. He grumbled. I left for the store.

*   *   *

Shopping took less than forty-five minutes, but it was enough time for David to pursue another one of his well-planned ideas. Walking into the house from the garage, I stood in amazement! The shock quickly turned to a little more than an annoyance. I found him literally ripping up the kitchen vinyl, plywood attached. Pushing the garage door closed behind me, I heard the doorbell. I set the groceries in David's recliner, yelling, "What are you doing? Are you out of your mind?"

The doorbell rang again. I took the few steps necessary to open the door. It was Jim, a hospice volunteer. Seeing him, I threw my hands in the air and pointed toward the kitchen. Nothing interrupted David's performance, not the doorbell or Jim's presence.

Jim, an Amish gentleman, had a grin and relaxed manner that could melt an iceberg. David took to him right away. Why wouldn't he? Jim would do whatever David wanted. They could sit in silence, which didn't happen very often, or talk about building a barn. It was all just fine. So it wasn't long before Jim became a true friend and his name a household word.

With his thumbs hooked in his jean pockets, Jim moseyed over to David, "I've got just the tool for you, David. It'll scrape that vinyl right off the floor, easy as pie. Why don't we sit and have some visit time and I'll bring the tool by tomorrow?"

Breathing in short gasps, David's flushed face expanded into a smile, a possible sign that all would be well for at least the next few hours. Jim came the next day as promised with a tool that had a shovel handle with a flat steel plate attached. He proceeded to scrape the vinyl off the floor, leaving enough small pieces for David to work on when he could.

My oldest daughter had arrived from Arizona a few days before the boys. She would start working on the wallpaper. When installed the paper had been prepared for easy removal, so the job would be a breeze I told her. After two days, she was still trying to steam the wallpaper off with an iron. She patiently picked at small pieces until she managed to remove about a three foot square. That left two hundred more to go. My boys arrived just in time to find their sister ironing the wall. They chuckled. They'd put their expertise into action with a commercial steamer and get the wallpaper to cooperate. But like everything else in those days, things became complicated. The paper had taken on a David-type stance. It intended to stay put. Absolutely nothing we could do changed its attitude: not sponging it, not scraping it, not using the steamer or even applying a chemical. David sat in his recliner with suction tubing in hand, watching the show. In the end it all turned out to be busywork in the ninety degree temperature. The paper had won.

I had given up. Somehow, through the grace of the good Lord, a neighbor who hung paper for a living came to our rescue. Poor fellow made the mistake of stopping to say hello, saw our predicament and told us the paper could be painted with a chemical and then papered over. He got hired.

"Forward" became the motto. The furniture I couldn't move was either covered with tarps or carried into an already well-stuffed garage. David, smiling like a kid on a swing, was moved, chair and all, to accommodate the work.

The power tools whined a different melody from each room as the boys embedded the screws into the floor boards. David supervised on his pad of paper.

The painting, both walls and ceilings, had to be done before the neighbor could hang the new paper. The kitchen vinyl had to be installed prior to the carpet. During the process fans were placed in strategic places and doors and windows opened to the maximum. The objective was to keep David and the rest of us breathing. By the time the walls were painted, the vinyl in, and the wallpaper painted with the chemical, we were all silly-willies. After doing an impossible job in two and a half days the family left, still happy for some strange reason.

As the wallpaper took more time than expected, I was behind schedule for the new carpet to be installed. Wouldn't you know: The carpet folks were ahead of schedule! I tried to explain the situation to the company.

"We got behind because we couldn't get the wallpaper off. The paperhanger will start early tomorrow morning. I would appreciate it if you could come later."

Talk about a deaf ear, his was worse than mine. Regardless, they would join the paper-hanger in the morning. The house turned into a blanket of carpet that went up the sides of cupboards and walls. The neighbor tried to limit his needed space, but the carpet people wanted it all. It became a war between the wooden horses, the planks for the wallpaper job and the carpet, for all available space. David sat calmly with tubing in hand on the new vinyl, watching the show.

By the time the remodeling had been completed, my heart raced constantly and my chest felt tight. I needed a few days away. I could find solitude with my friend, Phyllis, in Colorado Springs. Of course, it was a long drive from Indiana, but it was my best option. Before I could do anything, plans for David's care had to be made.

Hospice's respite program gave the caregiver five days for rest and relaxation. The patient would either be placed in a nursing home or the hospital, depending on where a bed was available. However, I didn't want to use my respite. I wanted to save it for an emergency in case I wouldn't be able to manage David's care. Then the five days would be a blessing, offering me some relief and financial aid.

With my goal of Colorado in mind, I once again looked for a place for David. Before I could do anything, David insisted he could stay alone. He refused to leave our home. I don't know why this came as a surprise. It was his typical pattern—surprises came with David. Sure that staying alone would be an act of insanity, I took him to his doctor. The doctor would certainly convince him that this would not be a good idea. I sat, very sure of myself, as I listened to the doctor question David.

"Can you still walk?"

David's upper torso bounced forward as he attempted to nod his head, "yes."

"Barely!" I countered.

"Then you can stay alone," he said as he swiveled his chair back to his desk.

Dumbfounded, I protested.

In a singsong manner, the doctor said, "All the law requires is that in case of a fire he could get out of the building without help."

The conversation was over. David had won. The nurse who had been my witness was flabbergasted.

"What do you intend to do?"

"I'm going to Colorado. I've had all I can take. I have to get some rest someplace. Look at him, David is healthier than I am. If he wants to be this pigheaded and inconsiderate then he can just do as he wants. I suggest we find a way to do this, because I am leaving."

David never budged with his decision, and I didn't either. I continued to prepare my things for the trip. I signed documents which gave hospice complete authority, even to use my respite if necessary. I provided the names and numbers of the couple who were willing to take him. I arranged for people to check on him and sit with him on a regular basis. Unbelievably, he promised to use the Lifeline and the TTY phone if he wasn't feeling well. He'd e-mail me as often as possible, so I would know how he was doing.

Am I fooling myself or is this actually going to work? If it will, why is the pain in my stomach telling me differently?

With David's history of rejection and acceptance, he wouldn't be alone for very long before he'd come to his senses. If he didn't, I'd have at least five days all to myself.

Chapter 12: The Trip

The day finally arrived for my departure. As soon as I closed the garage door I felt a sense of relief. The drive would be a hurried one, and yet relaxing, a change of pace. I hadn't seen Phyllis in a long time, so she was excited about my visit.

Reaching Sterling, Colorado, I began to feel ill. The gradual increase in altitude with the sun bearing down on the driver's side had caught up with me. Seeing a sign for a rest station by the chamber of commerce, I took the exit. The sign posted next to the chamber read four thousand four hundred feet. *I'm surprised the altitude is having such an effect. But then, what did I expect? I haven't given a thought to my own health beyond the constant buzzing in my head.* I reached for my cooler and began eating as much cheese as I could to stabilize my system. After an hour's rest, I felt the protein had done its job. As the rays of the sun were part of the problem, I'd provide some shade for myself before going back on the road. Opening the window on the driver's side, I took a small towel, lapped it over the top edge and closed the window. Now I had some shade and I could see the traffic through my side mirror. From that point on I took it easy. I didn't want to be worn out when I arrived in Colorado Springs. Knowing Phyllis, she'd have something planned.

I hadn't been at Phyllis's home for more than a few hours when a call came in. Phyllis handed me the phone, saying it was the hospice nurse. My first thought was that Joyce wanted to make sure I had arrived safely.

Then I heard her say, "David is very bad. We don't expect him to last through the night. We've hired a private duty nurse to stay with him until you get back."

Standing became difficult. Cold chills ran through my body.

My reply was grief-stricken, but strong. "Where do you think I am, next door? I could never get there in time. Why didn't you use my respite instead of hiring a nurse?"

"We couldn't. He refuses to leave the house."

Phyllis stood close, asking, "What is it?"

I muttered, "David is dying."

I don't remember hanging up the phone. Frantically, I began grabbing my belongings from the closet and the dresser. Unable to concentrate, I couldn't remember what I had brought or where I had put things. Many items had already been dispersed into other areas of the home, like the bathroom and the kitchen. I fretted that I'd leave something behind. My mind wouldn't remember. It was a blank to worldly possessions.

"You can't leave!" Phyllis pleaded. "It's too dangerous to be on the road in your condition. Please don't do this."

"I have to! I have to get back. Somehow the good Lord will get me there. Please don't worry. I'll be OK. I promise that before I leave, I'll do a meditation. Right now, I have to get the car packed."

Minutes later the phone rang again. I felt a scream mounting in my throat, had David died? I shook my head "no" as Phyllis handed me the phone. Her eyes saddened. Gloom was written on her face.

My voice sounded hollow when I said, "Hello."

It was Joyce. "I don't want you so upset that you can't drive. He's not that bad."

"What?" I gasped.

"You need to come back anyway because he's not allowing us to care for him."

Shocked by the callousness of the first call, I said, "How could you do this to me? I can barely stand up. Did you even consider what kind of an effect this would have on me? You should have thought of that before you told me he was dying. I gave you the authority to put him in respite. Are you telling me you can't do that?"

"Yes."

"With David's history of bullheadedness, you didn't know he could refuse your orders before I left? You didn't know this was a possibility? You should have known this! You should have known what to do if it happened. But it appears you don't know your own administrative policy, do you? How could you let me drive all this way for nothing?"

"I'm sorry, but we never expected him to refuse the care. None of that matters now. It's water over the dam. As you drive back, we are asking that you stop and let us know where you are."

My heart fluttered and pounded in my chest as I listened to the flat monotone in which she

60

delivered her demands. The receiver shook in my hand; I raised my left hand to steady it. I wanted to run away. I didn't want to talk to her any more. Nothing made sense. I felt the bed for a place to sit, but it was covered with suitcases.

"I have a hearing loss, remember? You want me to waste time looking for a phone I can understand on, so you will know where I am, for what? What will that accomplish? I have to pack to leave, goodbye."

Phyllis had done her best to gather my things. Again, she begged me not to leave.

"There's nothing you can do. There's no sense killing yourself over this. You have given hospice all the authority they need to handle any situation."

"I know, but it doesn't look like they plan to use it. The nurse said we would have to pay for the private duty nurse, and that'll be a lot. I'll have to leave, whether or not I want to. I'm sorry it didn't work out."

Before leaving I sat very still in a comfortable chair and closed my eyes. After a few deep breaths I imagined the azure water of the Pacific. My heart slowly returned to its normal rhythm, but the ordeal left me weak. *Perhaps I'll begin to feel better once I'm out of the altitude.*

The duty hospice imposed upon me caused me to worry about David's future care. I didn't know what would happen if I didn't follow the rules. Maybe I was being paranoid, but I couldn't chance it. I'd have to do as I was told.

On the way I stopped a couple of times, but I couldn't find a phone. It wasn't until I reached the motel at two-thirty in the morning that I was able to call.

Upon getting the nurse, I asked, "Is David in respiratory distress?"

After a pause she replied, "I don't know."

"You don't know?"

"Well, I don't have anything to compare it with. I don't know how he was before I got here."

"What!" I snapped. "I'm asking you if he is having trouble breathing."

"No…I don't think so."

"Are you a registered nurse?"

"Yes."

"Then go in and check him. I want to know his condition."

She returned to tell me that he was resting comfortably, a pat nursing response.

"Would you please let hospice know that I'm in Illinois? I should be home sometime late afternoon or early evening."

"I can't. They're not open now; and I go off duty at six this morning."

"Then ask the nurse coming on duty to call them."

"I can tell her, but I can't guarantee she'll call them."

After hanging up, my mind continued to do reruns of the conversation. I was tired, maybe she misunderstood.

A Reason to Dream

*How could a nurse not know how to answer
a question on respiratory distress? Couldn't a
layperson answer that one?*

Being beyond exhaustion, I couldn't sleep.
The cruelty of the first phone conversation with the
hospice nurse overwhelmed my thoughts. Unrelated
thoughts jumped the fence of logic.

*Did the nurse color the truth when she
called back? Would David be gone by the time I
returned? I bet she changed her story to calm me
down, so I wouldn't have an accident. Then they
wouldn't be responsible. Could I possibly make it
back in time? If I fall asleep I won't get an early
start. Then I'll miss him forever.*

Chapter 13: Life Goes On.

The next morning I woke with a start. The first light crested the sky as I drew the blind. I got dressed, groggy from minimal rest. Quickly, I grabbed the few things I had brought into the motel and jumped into the car. There wasn't time to dally.

A couple hundred miles down the road a red light flashed on the dashboard, "Check Motor." Terror struck my heart. The parched Nebraska land left few resources to a stranded motorist. I prayed that I'd make it to the next exit, some twenty miles away. *I don't need to be stuck alone on the highway in this heat.*

As soon as I reached the exit I felt safer. It would be good to be around someone, anyone. I pulled into the only filling station and asked the checkout lady for help. I paced outside in the heat while the clerk continued to take care of people who spent less than a dollar. Finally, an elderly man came out to help. He poked his head under the hood and, after ten minutes of tinkering with everything non-electrical, he decided the radiator needed water.

"If the light comes on again, ma'am, stop at the next exit. There's a Dodge dealership there. It's about forty miles down the road."

Back to praying! As the gentleman was the only help available, I continued on my way. Unfortunately, I had barely driven a mile when the light came back on. *Oh well, I only have thirty-nine miles to go in this ninety-five degree temperature. If the car dies, I'll probably join it as I'll be fried alive with very little water to put out the fire. Oh yes, I do have water in the radiator.* If ever I should have been arrested for speeding, it should have been then. I tried to concentrate on praying, but my eyes kept diverting to the dashboard, expecting something else to happen. Somehow, and I do believe through divine intervention, I made the forty miles.

Not having a clue as to the location of the dealership, I pulled into a carwash for directions. Every dirty car in the world sat in a typical "follow the leader" line. After I couldn't get the attendant's attention, I parked. He did his utmost to ignore me, turning away and talking to anyone within earshot. Having run out of patience, and being as tired as a bear awakened after a short winter's nap, I stepped in front of him.

"I have an emergency here."

"Lady, everybody in this line has an emergency."

I puffed up the little steam I had left and shouted, "My husband is dying."

Wanting to get rid of me in a hurry, he quickly gave me the directions to the Dodge dealership.

Arriving at the dealership, I asked to speak to someone in charge. The service tech got the owner. When I told him about my situation with David, he ordered other work stopped and mine completed. Within an hour, the fellows had diagnosed the problem and had me back on the road. My alternator and voltage regulator had died. I had driven the distance of sixty plus miles on my battery; to me it was a miracle.

Carolee O'Neill

I walked into the house later that day, dirty and bedraggled. David was sitting in his recliner, suction tubing in hand. As he sat up as straight as he could to greet me, I knew he was as good as could be expected. I didn't procrastinate. I discharged the nurse and called hospice to tell them I had arrived. I didn't know who to be angrier with, David, hospice, or myself. I shouldn't have left. I only dug a deeper hole. Now exhaustion would be a constant companion.

* * *

That night I chose to sleep in the finished lower level because the bed had fresh linens; the one upstairs had been stripped and I was too tired to make it. In the middle of the night my bladder decided it needed a potty break. I slid out of bed in the darkness. An icy sensation chilled my body. I was standing in water. A zillion thoughts flashed through my head. *Am I dreaming?* A shiver answered that question. *But where is it coming from? Oh Father, not something else!* I was smack in the middle of another disaster. I started to weep, not caring much about anything. Gradually, I made my way to the staircase. As my eyes adjusted to the dim light from the basement windows, minimal logic reminded me I needed to get out of the water before turning on the lights.

Reaching the staircase, which was in the middle of the basement, I climbed onto the first step. It felt dry, so I turned on the switch. The light shimmered across the wet floor. Half of the basement was flooded. The carpet had acted as a barrier, diverting a lot of the water toward the vinyl

66

under the bed. I looked back and forth across the room. The deepest water seemed to be coming from the furnace room. *The water heater must have sprung a leak. With all that had been going on, who would've thought to check a water heater?* I stepped wide onto a dry section of the carpet and headed for the laundry room to turn off the main. I realized that if I hadn't slept downstairs the whole basement would have flooded. I thanked our Father for putting me in the right place again. Then I ran up the stairs to wake David. He would know how to get the water up. Seeing the response on his pad, I thought he had lost his mind.

"Take the bag out of the Fairfax vacuum and reverse the draw, so you can suck up the water. Put a cloth around the metal wand so you don't get shocked. Don't touch the metal. Keep your hands on the cloth."

"Are you kidding me?"

"Just do it," he wrote, drawing a dark line under his words.

This had to be the craziest idea I had ever heard. Did my electrician know what he was talking about? He'd better. I had to do something about the water, and I didn't have many options in the middle of the night. I figured the worst thing that could happen was that I'd get a perm out of it; I did what he said. I began by sucking up the water on the vinyl. The rag slid a little with each movement of the wand. I grabbed it tighter. As I worked, I became nauseous from being overtired. I wanted to concentrate on how bad I felt, not on the job. I forced myself to focus. In spite of my efforts, a zombie-like daze captured my mind.

Suddenly, my hand slipped. A bolt of electricity vibrated through my arms, ending in my feet. You'd think that one good jolt would have put an end to this madness, but it didn't. Instead, I reminded myself that I had to pay closer attention. The warning kept me alert for another ten minutes. Then a second and a third jolt snapped me into reality. This was getting old fast. With zero probability that the water would go someplace, I decided to wait until eight in the morning and call the church for help. I grabbed a blanket out of the hall closet and headed for the sofa. After closing the door to the basement, I had no trouble falling asleep. I had been fried, frozen and frightened. What else could happen?

An hour after I called the next morning, three fellows came over, moved the furniture and sucked up as much water as they could with their shop-vacs.

Next I called Bob, the guy who never did get to pull up all the kitchen vinyl.

"Don't worry about a thing," he said. "I'll see that everything is taken care of."

Looking into the mirror the next morning shocked me more than the vacuum cleaner. Puffy eyes, the kind bagged with oceans of fluid, were accented by hair that preferred to stand up and out, rather than lay down. After that I pretty much decided to drag myself around in a daze after the fellows left.

A Reason to Dream

A little after lunch I received a call from Joyce, the hospice nurse. She said there were a couple of things that we needed to talk about. At ten o'clock the next day, she arrived with Jan, her supervisor.

In not a breath of time Jan began her reprimand, "We had this problem with David because you used the one eight hundred number," she scolded with a tight jaw. "Where did you get it?"

Not expecting the attack, I stuttered, "I-I don't remember. I think I got it from your aide. What difference does it make?"

"It just so happens that the call went to the hospital switchboard and they are not equipped to handle a TTY call. That meant David couldn't get help when he needed it."

"How am I supposed to know what you can and can't handle? The aide was trying to help us with long distance charges. Aren't you blaming us for one of your problems?"

David leaned forward in his chair, patting his chest as he attempted to moan out a sound. His body language was clear. He was trying to say that it was his fault. Then he wrote on his pad,

"Leave her alone."

"I'll tell you what we are going to do," Jan said. "We are insisting that you both obey all the rules and that includes not using the one eight hundred number. If you break one more rule, we will no longer handle David's case."

Quickly, Jan got up and walked out of the door with Joyce right behind her.

Sadness filled David's eyes as he wrote, "I'm sorry."

I nodded in acknowledgment and then stared blankly ahead, thinking, *I should have said, "Oh no, we didn't! We had this problem because your nurse didn't know her job. She hadn't prepared me for what could happen if David refused hospice care. My life became a living hell because of it. And what about telling me that he was dying?* But I didn't. As usual the thoughts surfaced after the battle. I curled up in my recliner to soothe my wounded spirit.

Between doctor appointments for David and preparing for hospice care, my mammogram had been overlooked. About the same time, I noticed that my driver's license was about to expire. Being considered high risk for breast cancer, I had to get that scheduled and also get my license.

Expecting a good report I waited patiently in the radiology department for the tech to tell me she didn't have to take any more films. Instead, my greatest fear surfaced. The mammogram showed a lump.

"We'll need to take more pictures and schedule you for an ultrasound," the technician said. "We should be able to get you in next week for the ultrasound."

Jarred by the unsettling news, I couldn't sleep, stop shaking, or stop crying. That didn't change the expiration date on my license. I had to take care of it, like it or not. Before I left the house, I told David I was going to renew my license. He grabbed his billfold off of his utility table and took out his license. Frantically, he pointed his finger

continually at his chest and then toward the outside
as he choked out a constant monotone with a gaping
mouth. I walked to his side, wondering why he was
making such a fuss.

He wrote on his pad, "My license, too."

I said firmly, "David, you can't drive
anymore. Standing in line will be a horrible
experience as weak as you are. Why do you want to
do this?"

He continued to thump on his pad until I
agreed to take him. Engulfed in my own misery
with the impending ultrasound, I didn't argue. A
handkerchief stuffed in his pocket and one in his
hand would work for his sputum wipes. Off we
went.

As usual the line was very long. I pulled out
chairs for David to sit on as we proceeded down the
aisle, but he refused. Then he'd falter. I'd grab a
chair. Horror filled the faces of people standing
close. David would regain his balance and falter
again. I'd grab another chair. People backed away,
putting a healthy distance between them and David.
This went on until I finally gave up and sat down.

*He can just be bullheaded and fall on his
duff. This is such a waste of time anyway. The
bureau isn't going to give him a license.*

When we reached the front desk, he
sheepishly laid his license on the counter and wrote,
"I need to renew."

The clerk smiled and pulled out the
paperwork, explaining to David how to fill it out. I
was thunderstruck. *She's going to do this?*

71

Carolee O'Neill

Picking up the license, she said, "Sir, your license is still good. You don't need a renewal."

He grinned. I groaned, and I took him home. Thank heaven, he didn't ask to drive. Perhaps he just wanted to know he hadn't lost another privilege. Or was it his sense of humor shining through? I wasn't sure I hadn't been the one taken for a ride.

The technician doing the ultrasound told me not to worry. "It's only a cyst. I see lots of these."

I sighed.

Three doctors didn't agree. I had to have a biopsy. *The tech seemed so sure, but I guess as much as I don't want to do this, I can't risk it.* The doctor's office scheduled the biopsy. Along with it, they gave me conflicting information as to how it would be done. First they said they would anesthetize the area. Then I was told they wouldn't. The thought of doing the procedure without anesthetic sent my emotions to outer space. When the doctor saw the look on my face, before he did the procedure, he ordered a sedative that would put my eyeballs back in their sockets and close my mouth. I waited, an hour went by. By the time they had me set up in the mammogram machine, I looked like something out of a horror movie. The needle went in—a milky fluid ran out. The ultrasound tech was right. My tumor turned into a plugged milk gland. I turned into a basket case.

A Reason to Dream

Chapter 14: One Last Visit

As suspected, the home repairs had a detrimental effect on David's health. After I returned from Colorado, his breathing became labored and his body appeared more rigid. To complicate matters, a neighbor made sure she filled me in on one of David's other activities.

"David is hiding in the bushes on the side of the house, smoking. You have to stop him."

Fat chance! David had been smoking for sixty years, as though I could stop him. Was it a surprise? Hardly! On several occasions I thought I smelled the familiar odor of cigarettes, but felt it was my imagination. It would be insane for a man with all his health problems to be smoking. After the visit from the neighbor, I knew better.

In the midst of this madness, I thought if I took him to see his pulmonary specialist there might be a slim chance the doctor could convince David to stop smoking.

The chubby, red in the face doctor did not mince his words. "By far, your pulmonary condition is a bigger threat to you right now than the ALS," he said as he pounded his finger on David's chart. "You'd better listen to me if you want to live!"

As usual, David didn't heed the doctor's words. The best thing would be to let it go. At this point he couldn't control much of anything, other than his smoking. Only the good Lord knew how long that would be. So he continued to hide in the bushes until he couldn't draw on a cigarette.

73

Carolee O'Neill

*   *   *

Managing David's pain became an endless challenge. Many times his medicine couldn't be given through his stomach tube because of the residual (excessive fluid). Putting it in his mouth didn't work, either. With a paralyzed throat, David would choke or it would run out of his mouth. Repeatedly, I asked Joyce for some pre-filled syringes.

With the syringes, I can give him an injection of morphine to control his pain.

I had no idea why they ignored my requests. Their refusal catapulted our situation toward hardship.

A couple of weeks after I had returned from Colorado, David's granddaughter, Heather, and her husband, Tim, came for a visit. They were bringing David's new great-granddaughter. It would be an exciting time for both of us as we had not seen any family for several months. I didn't tell him about the expected visit. Shortly before they arrived, I straightened his bedding and brought up the head of his bed. When Heather entered the room with the baby, David's gaunt face hid behind a grin that made his eyes sparkle. Gently, Heather placed baby Rose next to her great-grandpa. He sat looking at her for several minutes: her tiny fist grasped his finger and his heart.

Suddenly, David pushed himself to the edge of his bed. Heather grabbed the baby. David motioned toward his pad. I quickly handed it to him. He wrote "bathroom." Just as fast, he dropped his pad, his eyes glazed, and his body became rigid.

74

I sat down on the bed next to him. Placing my arm around his shoulder, I assured him I wouldn't leave him. I helped him with the urinal and then asked him to try and lay back on the pillows. When he didn't move, I tried to move him, but I couldn't budge him. Afraid he would slide off the edge of the bed, I called to Heather and Tim. Slowly, we were able to move his rigid body and get him back in bed. While they stayed with him, I called hospice.

I can't wait for the nurse to arrive. I have to try to medicate him.

My hands trembled as I readied his medication.

He is in so much pain. Don't look at David. Get a hold of yourself. No! No! I can't do this. I only have the two routes and neither of them is any good. But I have to do something. I'll try his stomach tube first.

After inserting the syringe, I pulled back on the plunger to remove the residual, but nothing happened. *It's not working.*

My strength met with an immovable resistance.

The tube must be lodged against his stomach wall. I'll have to try his mouth.

The medicine ran out of his mouth and on to his gown. The sadness in David's eyes told me he understood what I was doing. I tried the stomach tube again, but all attempts were futile. There was nothing I could do.

David shouldn't have to suffer like this. I should have pushed harder for the syringes.

75

Ravaged by guilt, yet angered by my lack of options, I shouted, "I don't know why they couldn't give me those syringes, David. I'm so sorry you are going through this. There's no reason why you should have to suffer like this."

With great effort, he raised his hand and stroked my face. I took his hand in mine, caressing it against my tear-streaked face.

"Honey," I whispered. "I've called hospice. The nurse is on her way. I won't leave you."

Heather and Tim came in to say goodbye for the last time. She touched his hand, but only his eyes reflected the softness of his heart.

*   *   *

The hospice nurse on call happened to be within a mile of our home. Cell phone to her ear, she walked through the house listening to instructions from her supervisor.

"They told me to put his medication in his mouth," she said as she snapped her phone shut.

"That doesn't work. I just tried and it ran out."

I watched as she repeated the same procedure with the same results.

"We'll have to admit him to the hospital. I'll call an ambulance. You won't be billed because hospice is given three days for emergencies like this."

She popped open her cell phone and began organizing the transfer. Quickly, we were lost in business tasks, the necessary procedures that keep the medical professional oblivious to the patient's reality.

"We'll have to get one of those pumps installed," she said, "That'll handle his pain."

"What pump?" In disbelief I listened as she told me about a subcutaneous pump. David could push a button when he needed the medication and it would be delivered.

"Why hasn't this been done for him a long time ago?"

"I don't know, but I will do my best to get it put in as soon as we get to the hospital."

Moments later the ambulance arrived with its lights flashing, warning the neighborhood of our dilemma. The emergency medical techs lifted David onto a gurney in a sitting position. I grabbed as many of his things as I could: bathrobe, slippers, comb and razor. As the ambulance pulled out of the driveway, I started the car to follow them. I'd have to take care of his admission before I could go to him.

A foul odor penetrated the air as the elevator opened onto the fourth floor of the hospital. I gagged. Covering my nose and mouth with a handkerchief, I wondered how David could breathe in that atmosphere.

By the time David got to the room, he didn't seem so rigid. I assumed he had been medicated. Pulling the overstuffed chair to his bedside, I held his hand.

"Try to get some rest, honey. I will sit here for awhile."

The sky had darkened by the time David had fallen asleep. It would be a long drive home, so I needed to get on my way. The night seemed exceptionally black, or was it? I stared into the night without emotion. Headlights flashed by, stinging my eyes as I wondered if the last hours had really happened. Under the rush of hurried decisions time became a whisper. The noise of machines had gradually faded into the background of my life. The medical profession's schedules became who I was and it would stay that way until the end.

A Reason to Dream

Chapter 15: Control

I got to the hospital the next morning around
nine. I ran into Joyce who took me by the arm and
led me into a private room. Feeling I didn't have a
choice, I stood listening to her. Coolly, she drilled
me on what I should and shouldn't say to David.
They didn't want him to know what they were
going to do. Then he wouldn't be able to refuse
their orders. For the second time, I felt like her fist
had tightened around my heart when she said they
didn't expect him to last three days.

"Should I have him admitted to Hospice
House in St. Joe County?"

"No!" she said shortly. "But you will have
to look for a nursing home in this area in case he
lasts longer than expected. One thing for sure, he
will not be going back home. We don't want him to
know that."

A myriad of questions ran through my head.
*Why can't he go home? If we have the pump, I can
take care of him. I thought hospice patients were
supposed to die at home. Why are they doing this?
Why is she telling me to find a nursing home, if they
don't expect him to live?*

Hurt and confused, I prayed David wouldn't
ask me any questions when I got to his room. I
wouldn't lie to him. Somehow God would show me
the way.

When I got to David's room, I noticed he
had scribbled a short note on his pad.

Picking up the pad I read, "I want to say
goodbye. I don't know how long I will last."

79

Carolee O'Neill

I couldn't lift my eyes to meet his. If I did I would have to say goodbye. He didn't look different than he did a week ago, so how could he be dying? I remembered a neighbor telling him how good he looked. David wrote, "You can't see this disease."

I'm probably blinder to it than anyone. Hospice keeping me buried in endless tasks, and seeing to David's needs kept my mind off of the inevitable. I didn't have time to think.

My hand shook as I picked up his hand and kissed it. "I love you, honey."

At that moment it was all I could say.

Mixed fears ravaged my heart; I'd be alone. What will I do without him? I sat holding his hand for a long time, then said, "It won't be long before I'll be with you. Time goes by so quickly."

Slowly, he nodded and pointed at me.

My eyes filled with tears, "Don't worry about me. I'll be OK. Don't hang on for my sake, David. You do what you need to do."

The second hospital day, I told David I had been looking for a nursing home. Most of them reeked of urine and overcooked food, but I did find one possibility. A sexy brunette from the home I liked would come to the hospital to interview him.

I saw a twinkle in his eye that told me he approved.

He wrote, "Don't worry about the care I get. I'll never get the care you gave me."

Our eyes met. No smile present, only sorrow.

"Thank you, honey."

*　　*　　*

The minister came to visit in the afternoon, asking why I hadn't put David in Hospice House in St. Joe County.

"The hospice nurse told me not to. Besides, if I did, David wouldn't have a doctor. We've already had to change doctors because the first one wouldn't prescribe morphine. One of its side effects is depressed respiration. His doctor didn't want any part of that. That's when the hospice nurse got a doctor who would prescribe it."

"David belongs in Hospice House. I don't know why they would tell you such a thing. Don't worry, Hospice House has the connections to get David whatever he needs."

Torn between the minister's words and the possibility of David not getting care, I procrastinated. With him in a good nursing home I wouldn't have to worry about his care.

Two days are gone and David still doesn't have the pump.

Several times a day I questioned the hospital staff, but without success. I'd be told it would be done that day, but it never happened. I resorted to everything from begging to demanding, anything that might get their attention. Then other concerns surfaced. He hadn't had a bed bath, or any personal care. They had left him alone. No one came to help him to the bathroom. After repeated attempts with the call button, David tried to get there on his own, an impossible feat. Consequently, he fell twice within the three day stay. I wondered why they

81

didn't hang a sign on his door that read, "This patient is dying, so you can forget about him."

After badgering the nursing staff, they finally told me the hospice aides were supposed to take care of David. He was their patient.

"Why didn't you tell me that right away? I could have done something."

"We assumed you knew. We try not to interfere with what hospice does."

My professional voice became stiff along with the hairs on the back of my neck. "If I knew, please tell me why I kept asking you questions about his care. Does that really make sense to you? If it does, I don't want you ever to provide care for me." I turned my back in defiance and walked away.

I don't know why I thought I could get better care for David. Every day was an uphill struggle. I hadn't even been effective with getting the pump for him. Regardless, I tracked down Joyce.

"Scheduling David's care seemed to have gotten lost in the paper shuffle," she chuckled.

Her response was ghostly to my soul. *Keep your eye on the end of the tunnel; Phyllis always said that when things got rough. Hospice isn't telling me anything, so I have no way to prepare for the next assault. I'll have to take matters in my own hands, as much as possible.* I made arrangements with the nursing home that had interviewed David. His care would remain the same until I could get him transferred. Then I could control his care. For that I didn't need anyone's permission.

The days were long, yet ended quickly. The sun blazed its rays into David's room in the morning and left a chill in the afternoon.

As I walked into his room that afternoon, fear laden emotions caused me to tremble. David was squirming in his bed, trying to groan out a cry. When he looked towards me, his face was distorted, his mouth agape and his eyes wide.

I ran to his side, "What's the matter, David?"

He put his hand on his chest and then pointed upward.

"Are you afraid of dying?"

He nodded.

I held him close, "David, nothing could be as bad as what you are going through."

The words seemed to calm him. Or maybe it was the embrace. It didn't matter.

Sadly, the pump had not been put in by the third day. All the energy I had used in its pursuit had been wasted. He would be transferred to the nursing home in the afternoon. My orders were to go home and transport his equipment, personal belongings and necessary furniture. The orders were explicit, more robotic chores that kept me from being with David. I'd have to get to the admissions office before they transferred him or the nursing home wouldn't let him in. I no longer believed that anything I did would get David better care with this hospice. However, I continued to do as I was told. I couldn't take a chance that hospice would drop him completely.

Once I got home, I gathered the most important things. While doing so, I noticed respiratory therapy had delivered the wrong tubing for the suction machine. What I had didn't fit the nozzle on his machine. Immediately, I called Joyce and told her to make sure the nursing home got the right tubing.

"What happened to the tubing you had?" Joyce asked.

"I put it in the garbage when he was taken to the hospital."

"Do you still have the garbage?"

"I . . . think so."

"Then take it out of the garbage and bring it with you."

"I can't believe you told me to do that. I won't do that. This is ridiculous. You have orders for David. Call respiratory therapy for the right tubing."

Joyce mumbled something I couldn't understand, so I hung up.

Grumbling about the suggestion, I put the top down on my 1985 Mercedes Roadster to make loading easier. By the time I finished, the car looked like something out of a Ma and Pa Kettle cartoon: table legs were pointing upward, walker legs downward, the utility table was on top of the television, the suction machine was in the back corner, and a couple of suitcases fit securely between the rest. The convertible accommodated everything beautifully, but the 90 degree temperature did little for my welfare.

As I pulled the car around to the rear entrance of the nursing home, I spotted a respiratory therapy truck in the driveway. Frantically, I jumped out of the car and ran over to the driver.

"Have you delivered David's tubing?"

Dumbfounded, the driver stood staring at me, "I don't know what you're talking about, ma'am."

I insisted he give me some tubing.

"I can't do that, ma'am, without an order. Besides, I wouldn't know what tubing to give you."

Seeing a nursing assistant inside the back door, I hurried toward her. I asked her to find a nurse immediately. She went inside and returned with a nurse. Explaining the situation with the tubing, the nurse assured me they had many different types of tubing. Certainly they'd have the right kind for David's machine.

"David will be arriving soon. We'll help you get his things into his room so you can get to the office and register him."

The paperwork took longer than expected because of the small print on the numerous contracts. Everything had to be read and signed, especially the check. I knew they wouldn't reject David as long as they had the money in their hands. With David admitted, I felt relaxed. He'd finally get some quality care, and he had a private room. As soon as my signature was on their last document, I walked toward his room.

As I approached I saw three staff members in what appeared to be a heated debate. One woman caught my eye, turned back to the others and then pointed at me. They rushed to my side, firing questions.

"When was he fed last?"

"Do you know when he had his last medication, and how much?"

"What about his oxygen and suction tubing? Where's the tubing? We don't have the right kind."

I rushed into David's room to find him attempting to jerry-rig his suction machine so he wouldn't choke to death on his sputum. He had arrived at the nursing home without a nurse, no doctor's orders, no tubing for his suction machine, no oxygen and no medication.

"Get some suction tubing in here right now," I screamed. "Any kind!"

I sat next to David, telling him to lean forward as much as he could. I hoped the sputum would drain from his mouth instead of running down his throat. The head nurse returned quickly with some tubing that we managed to squeeze onto the port of the machine. I dug through the luggage I had packed, handing the nurse some medication and the formula for his feeding.

An hour later Joyce arrived, laughing like a giddy teenager about being detained. Her attitude robbed me of words. What could I say that would make things better?

In the end, it took seven days to get the pump put in. By then, David wasn't able to push the button. New orders for an automatic pump would have to be gotten. That took two more days. Being in a good nursing home didn't mean a thing. He faced the same poor care, and the same poor scheduling. He was still under the same hospice.

The tears no longer came. My insides were as dead as David's. The only thought that continued to surface was to admit him to Hospice House in our county.

I don't understand. If they don't expect him to live, why are they telling me not to have him admitted to Hospice House? I don't care what they think anymore.

I went to Hospice House in St. Joseph County unannounced. I needed to see if what I had heard was true. The smell of fresh laundry lingered in the air. Each patient had a private room, and they were immaculate. A full kitchen had been provided for family members and sleeping arrangements were available. I went back to their front desk and requested an appointment to be interviewed. The next morning, the nurse in charge of admissions called. It was Ann, a young woman whom I had sold a home to fifteen years prior. I told her about David's situation and she agreed to meet me at the nursing home the next day.

Chapter 16: The Final Insult

David was in a fetal position when I walked into his room the next morning. I put my hand over my mouth to muffle my sobs. My beloved had been through another ordeal. His head and face were badly bruised, and his arms and hands looked as though someone had cut him with a razor blade.

The hospice aide's voice quivered as she spoke. "This happened earlier this morning. Before I got here," she added quickly. "They said he was trying to get up and knocked down a glass bottle. I guess he fell into the glass."

Sadness broke the final strand of congeniality left in my soul. Emotions stayed buried, nothing moved. Time rambled by silently, without awareness. It seemed somebody outside of me wanted answers, but couldn't ask. Before sound broke forth, a far away voice echoed in my head. Then Ann's words broke into my thoughts.

"How long has he been like this?"

Staring at David, I whispered, "I don't know. . . I just found him."

In a singsong tone the aide smiled and said, "I put a diaper on him, so he should be comfortable now. At least he won't have to worry about getting up."

Silence again held the room in its grasp. My usual "thank you" did not come. The final insult had been delivered, a diaper.

Ann broke the silence, saying we needed to talk about David's transfer. Guilt surfaced as she

described the care he would receive at Hospice
House.

*I let him down. I shouldn't have followed
orders. I should have done something sooner.*

"All you have to do is call an ambulance to
pick David up in the morning," Ann said. "We will
do everything possible to keep him comfortable."

It was around five in the afternoon when
Ann left. David had not responded. I kissed him on
the forehead and whispered, "Honey, tomorrow
morning I'm having you transferred to Hospice
House.

It is such a beautiful facility and the people
are so compassionate. I can stay with you overnight,
so you'll never be alone. You'll finally get the care
you deserve."

I drove home with the picture of my
wounded husband in my mind. No longer could I
question why it happened. It didn't matter. It
happened.

As soon as I got home I made arrangements
for the ambulance, but it was in vain. I had just
hung up when the nursing home called. David had
died. He went peacefully, they said, in his sleep. I
called my friend, Bob. He drove me to the nursing
home. The minister would meet us there.

Entering the room, the night light accented
the dreariness as I walked to David's side. I felt
nothing, not even a tear filled my eyes. I stared at
the ghostly, ashen body that lay before me, cold to
my touch. A dropped jaw had elongated the thin
bluish face. Eyes that wouldn't close in sleep,
feigned an empty stare. I told myself it really wasn't

David. It couldn't be David. It didn't look like him. I placed my hand on his forehead as though it would answer my questions.

Warmth touched my other hand. The minister had taken it. We should gather by the bed while he prayed. It didn't take very long, less than a minute. Seemed strange to pray for such a short while for a lifetime of living, but then, did it really matter?

"Death isn't a very pretty sight," the minister said.

Captured by indifference, I turned and began gathering David's things. No words were spoken as Bob carried the boxes to his car.

When we finished, I stood next to the bed. *Why did you die now? I finally found a good place for you. Didn't you want to go to Hospice House where you'd be safe—where you wouldn't be alone? Instead, you went and died on me.*

I jumped as someone's hand touched mine. "I'm sorry, but I have to leave," the minister said. "There's another family who needs me down the hall. Call me if you need anything."

A polite goodbye was uttered as I looked at David. *Maybe it was time to go home.*

You suffered too much with the poor care and the last transfer. Oh dear God, was another one more than you could bear?

I gasped at the thought and my stomach soured. *Maybe it's a good thing you died. Isn't it always a good thing when people die? It's over with. You're not suffering any longer.*

The thoughts were as empty as David's eyes. They were the things we tell ourselves to ease our burden, to force ourselves away from the reality of death.

Chapter 17: Staying Put

After David died, I joined a grief support group at my church. Upon arriving for the meeting, a façade of congenial ambiance filled the room with small talk about activities attended, but nothing about how we actually felt. Jan, the moderator, asked us to be seated. Every week the small group of eight or ten received handouts and books that covered the grieving process. These were heavily laden with reminders of the past. Our assignment was to acknowledge our feelings and write down any personal growth we had achieved during the week. One of the books, which I had already read, was "Death and Dying" by Dr. Kubler Ross.

Staring at the cover, my mind reverted to the heaviness that hung over the loveseat I sat on a few feet from the casket. It was the proper place for the family of the departed to meet with the few people that came to offer their condolences. Those who did shared little and disappeared quickly. Sounds of mumbled prayers and whispered stories about David's disease mingled with nervous laughter. I felt as though my head was in a box that dimmed the light with a haze. I began to question if David had ever been alive, but the pinstripe suit that had flattered his physique lay collapsed, proving his departure. His glasses hung cockeyed on the bridge of his nose, giving the impression they were a substitute. I couldn't grasp the happenings as I sat waiting for something, not knowing what. Then a hand touched mine and someone said, "You've really had a rough time, haven't you?"

An old friend gazed softly into my eyes. Tears escaped.

Tenderly, he had wiped a tear with his thumb. "With the trauma you've been through maybe it would be a good idea to join a grief support group. I know there are some good ones. At least it's something to think about."

I had thanked him and wondered if anything could fill the hole left by David's absence.

Reality slapped me back when the moderator's piercing voice broke into what I had committed to memory, "This may be difficult for some of you because you have recently lost your loved one. But it's necessary so you can deal with your grief," Jan said.

My muscles tensed and my heart began to pound as I thumbed quickly through the pages of the book she had given us.

How dare she tell me what I have to do? I don't care how natural death is or what the stages of dying are. I just don't care about any of it. How am I supposed to do this? I don't think my friend knew what he was talking about when he told me to join a group.

"Who would like to start reading the first chapter?" Jan asked.

I can't do this. I can't even read a recipe right now. These other people must have lost their spouses some time ago, so maybe they can. I'll just sit here until it's time to go. After I get home it might not seem so bad.

Week after week an undercurrent of gloom took refuge in the conversations that no one could

93

get beyond. The same stories, the same feelings flourished. I began to wonder why I was alive. Listening to the people, I again felt darkness pull me into the depths of despair. To cope, I found myself taking over Jan's job, diverting the conversation to happy moments, telling jokes, anything to break free and reclaim my life.

The leaves were beginning to turn when a friend mentioned I shouldn't be alone over the holidays. I thought again of my friend Phyllis in Colorado. She'd been begging me to come for a visit. I could spend the first part of December with her, going to Christmas concerts and luncheons at the country club. Then I'd go to my daughter's home in Tucson for the winter. The trip would give me a way to leave the group gracefully and not be alone during the holidays.

A Reason to Dream

Chapter 18: Memories.

Even though it had been eight months since David died, the silence of driving back to Tucson from Canyon Lake, Arizona, caused the past to spring into my mind like a panther seeking its prey. I needed to think of ways to break this pattern. Thoughts of David's final days wouldn't lead me into the future. A quick stop might help me focus on something, like the beauty of the setting sun. I pulled over to the side of the road.

Stepping out of the car, I breathed deeply. The fresh mountain air felt cool to my lungs. I began to stroll along the roadside, gazing into the depths of a canyon polka-dotted with green shrubs and saguaro cacti. The sun had begun to hide behind the rusty colored mountains, casting shadows of gray and black on the desert sand. I kicked a stone and watched it tumble into the brush. It had been a beautiful day, warm for the mountains, but it was gone just like the stone. It seemed as though I had just started out on this trip moments ago. Now the fading light reminded me that the day was almost over.

Years ago, I remember hearing something profound that Norman Vincent Peale was supposed to have said. It was that dying and being born were similar. We don't remember either experience, but both encounters send us on a new journey.

I told myself that David had begun his new journey. He was with our heavenly Father. That's what I needed to hold on to, and the beautiful melody God had given us to share. With this in mind, I could continue on. Tucson slept less than a hundred miles away.

Suddenly, car lights flashed from around a curve. The car swerved and pulled off the road, parking in front of me. "You OK?" a man hollered.

A shudder surged through my body as I realized how insane it was to be walking in the desert alone. "Yes, thank you. I'm just enjoying the view."

"I wouldn't hang around these parts too long after the sun goes down, ma'am. There are a lot of wild animals in these mountains. Besides, the road gets pretty tricky after dark."

"Thank you," I hollered back. "I'll be careful."

He waved and was gone in a flash.

I watched his taillights until they disappeared, so fast, so final. My time with David had fled this way. Yet, living those days the moments hadn't been fleeting. Standing alone on the mountain with the early evening breeze caressing my face, I realized a whole lifetime had passed in a flash, like a whisper on the wind.

After spending time with my daughter over the holidays, I moved into a park model at The Voyageur RV campground the first of January. Being a little south of Tucson, I traveled between my daughter's home and The Voyageur for family gatherings.

Palm trees accented by flood lights, flower beds and real grass adorned the entrance to the park. The streets were filled with seniors going to or from the many activities The Voyageur sponsored. I decided to join something fun. That would help fill the loneliness that haunted my moments, without a tear. So I went to the activity department to see what would spark my interest.

I was surprised to see they had a grief support group. Thinking that perhaps it might be more upbeat, I thought I'd give it a try, along with the early morning exercise class. Perhaps the warmer days would help me see things differently.

At the first meeting of the support group we were told to buy a book on grieving that carried an expensive price tag. Being a newcomer to the group, I was too embarrassed to say no or to walk out. So I paid for the book. Later that evening I read the assigned chapter, questions at the end needed to be answered. The results had been the same, a deepening depression, but still no tears. As I was leaving the park in a couple of weeks, I used it as an excuse not to continue. With all the activities offered by the park, I planned to use my moments doing things that brought happy thoughts, like the exercise class.

Chapter 19: A New Day

The exercise class gave me an opportunity to mix with seniors who were living their dreams. Bound to keep up with people who were older than I, and moving much better, I did my one-two-three-fours and stretches. All I could think of was how much pain they caused.

Hearing me groan, the fellow behind me said, "It'll get better after awhile, just stick with it."

I smiled politely and wondered if I'd survive that long.

Before class the fellows gathered to share war stories about their rigs. I had considered owning a motor home, but being alone, I discounted the idea. Yet, I found their conversations intriguing. David's adventures with my son Chris as they panned for gold, urged me on. Listening to the fellows in class gave the possibility of ownership another boost. Here was a golden opportunity to move forward with my life. I didn't want to waste another moment.

Casually, I worked my way between a couple of brawny, six-foot fellows who towered over me by eight inches. It was a painless way to explore owning a motor home, with no strings attached. When conversation waned within the group, which wasn't often, I'd politely raise a question or two and tell them about my make-believe dream. Spurred by their macho nature, most of the fellows were anxious to answer my questions. After all, it wasn't every day they met a mature woman who might actually buy a motor home and travel on her own.

When I wasn't talking to the fellows about their rigs, I was riding my mountain bike through the motor home section, reminiscing about past travels. One afternoon, while I was out on my bike, a Pleasure Way van passed me. Its glossy white exterior glistened as the sunlight glanced off its nineteen-foot side.

Now there's something I could handle.

Wondering what it looked like inside, I decided to find out. I began my pursuit.

The fifteen mile an hour speed limit should keep it in view.

Nevertheless, it took every ounce of energy I could muster to keep up. Questions popped into my head as I shifted gears and pedaled faster than I knew possible. *I wonder how much something like that costs? It doesn't look like it would have enough storage space. The gas mileage has to be better than the Class A's or even the Class C's for that matter. Whatever I considered, I have to be able to do it on social security and the small pension David left me. That could get tricky.* The van made a right turn several streets ahead. Concerned I would lose it, I pedaled harder. When I rounded the corner, I saw it pull into a driveway at the far end of the street. In spite of my legs begging for relief, I continued my pace. I wanted to arrive at the home before the folks went inside. Barely able to catch my breath, I pulled into their driveway.

These folks are going to think I'm crazy or else the most brazen woman in the world.

Carolee O'Neill

An elderly lady with a curious smile slid out of the driver's side as I dismounted my bike. Returning the smile, I noticed an impish gleam in her eyes. Gentle lines embraced the smooth skin on her face as she stood fiddling with the keys in her hand. Promptly, the passenger's door opened. The sight of a cane emerged, followed by a gentleman with a quizzical look on his face. I introduced myself and told them I had lost my husband and I was looking for a way to move forward with my life, and I was impressed with their unit. The lady's interest sparked; she graciously offered to give me a tour. Walking through the coach, I remembered David's words. I'd need something bigger, especially if I planned to live in it for five or six months out of the year.

After the tour I listened to Esther. For years this agile, bright-minded, eighty-year-old lady had been driving their coach back and forth from Washington State to Tucson, Arizona, with her invalid husband. Inspired by her example, the idea of following this dream seemed like a possibility that could thrill my soul.

The months that followed were filled with learning about motor homes of all sizes and shapes. I had a reason to dream, to leap forward into the future and travel the country. Vibrant meadows where antelope grazed would capture my gaze. I could stand in awe of rugged, snow-packed peaks that released their crystal waters in the glimmer of the sun. I could hear the azure waters of the Pacific call my name through the whispering wind. A loving Father had placed the future in my hands.

A Reason to Dream

Chapter 20: Epilog

After living those moments with David, I wanted to do something different with my remaining years. I knew life was indeed short. Hoping to inspire others to go on after a loss I purchased a thirty-two foot Gulf Stream motor home by July 2002 and a car to tow a year later. I traveled by myself to touch the hearts of those who might need a word of encouragement. However, as it turned out, the rewards were mine.

For six years, I managed to avoid the grieving process as I trekked along in the motor home. The daily challenges kept me too busy to grieve the loss of my loved one. By April 2005, I had put almost twenty-six thousand miles on the motor home's odometer. With a trusting attitude and lack of experience, I learned to manage the camper (mostly by error), maintain various systems (in a unique way), stand up for my rights against the world, and that everything comes apart on a camper, but not always at the right time. More importantly, I learned there are more eagles in the world than turkeys. My profound hearing loss coupled with being a neophyte in the motor homes' arena turned my adventure into a comedy of hindsight with a glimmer of foresight.

Then a decision had to be made. As I was getting up in years, my brother told me I needed to be closer to my children. With that suggestion, I proceeded to pack, lift boxes and move furniture until nature had the final word. I became crippled with arthritis. Fearing surgery because of a long list

101

of drug reactions, I procrastinated. However, I continued to pray for an answer. As I did, I remembered God never gives us more than we can handle nor fails to provide a way out. Maybe surgery was my way out.

I had been blessed with a good primary care physician when I moved to Wisconsin, but would I have the same luck with a surgeon? Considering this, I temporarily escaped surgery by rationalizing perhaps God wanted me in a wheelchair to do His work. The pain answered that question. I was forced to see my doctor. She ordered x-rays to confirm her suspicions. "There's nothing left of your hip joints. No wonder you're in so much pain. I know a surgeon I'd like you to interview."

I trembled at the thought. Seeing my reaction, she said, "If you don't like him, I'll find someone else. You don't have to make a decision right now. Let's see what the surgeon has to say."

Surgery for a total hip replacement (THR) had changed dramatically since I had been in nursing. I headed for the medical library to find the latest research. Armed with two pages of questions and two pages of information I saw the surgeon.

To my surprise, the surgeon didn't try to convince me to have the surgery. Instead he lounged at his desk, patiently answering my questions. While he talked, I prayed for guidance. By the time he had finished, the options were clear. I'd either have the surgeries, or I would spend the rest of my life in a wheelchair.

Toward the end of the conversation, the surgeon mentioned he was a Christian.

My first reaction was, "Yeah sure!" A few days later, I ran into a friend who had the same surgeon for her knee.

"You're never going to believe this, but just before surgery he'll come to your side and pray with you."

Dumbfounded by her remark, I realized the surgeon had calmly provided the right answers; his bedside manner was impeccable, and he had the expertise to perform these surgeries. I had no reason to doubt him; I agreed to the surgery.

Just before the anesthesiologist was about to send me to la-la land, my surgeon showed up to pray for both of us. I had been blessed with an incredible personal physician and this surgeon to heal my broken body.

Three days after the first surgery, I was sent to a nursing home for rehab. It was an immaculate home and the staff was caring and efficient. As the hospice wing bordered rehab, the hospice patients would often join us for meals in the main dining room. As a result, we quickly became friends.

One day, the woman who sat across from me told the group she had developed an infection in her surgical hip, something we all feared. We prayed that the antibiotic would work, but it didn't. The infection spread to her shoulder, putting her back in the hospital to have the prosthesis removed and replaced at a later date. I feared for her life.

In the meantime, the drama played out before me. Hospice patients paraded the halls, a huge hospice banner draped above the kitchen counter, the families gathered in the main lounge to hear the disturbing news about their loved ones. My emotions were being dragged into their happenings. I started to cry about everything. Nightmares filled my dreams. The staff became concerned that I was depressed. I argued that I wasn't—I was worried about my friend. That's why I was crying.

I couldn't look at the oncology patients without crying. I couldn't watch television without crying. I couldn't think of my friend without crying. I needed to get out of the nursing home, no matter what my condition. The doctor signed the discharge papers and sent me home, but that didn't change anything. I continued to cry.

It wasn't until a few weeks had passed that I realized my friend's infection had triggered my grieving process. I had chosen to hide my pain by keeping busy, but the hospice signs and the patients took me back to the terror that had been locked in my heart.

Three months after the first surgery, I had the second hip done. The next months were filled with healing my spirit, grieving for my losses and learning to appreciate my growth. My Bible became a source of comfort. Placed within view, it reminded me daily that David was in a much better place with our Father. I allowed myself to cry and acknowledge my feelings, a tidbit I chose to ignore when told by both support groups. I began to talk freely about David, savored his poetry and wrote volumes about our fondest memories. Things like the truck mirror hitting the side of the RV, going to church on Christmas Eve with the Kleenex stuffed in his mouth, the gifts of love we shared in the dimness of the tree lights after the service, and the vision of him tearing up the vinyl off the kitchen floor—priceless.

Appendix 1: Hearsay and Fact

1. Hearsay: I questioned a nurse not connected with hospice about the prefilled syringes. I was told the hospice we were working with was under the guideline of a hospital. They were governed by hospital policy whose concern was that the drugs could get out on the street.

2. Fact: If I had known about these guidelines and discharged this hospice, they would have lost the revenue connected with the case. I was never informed of these guidelines.

3. Hearsay: With the trip to Colorado, I asked the opinion of an individual who had been involved with hospice for many years. The comment was that by leaving, I had made hospice the caregiver. This violated our contract with them.

4. Fact: However, prior to the trip this was never mentioned.

5. Fact: The problem in both instances was poor communication or a lack of communication.

6. Fact: One of the nurses was assigned to do follow-up with me for one year. I was aware that this was the rule. However, the nurse told me she hadn't been assigned. Exactly one year later, I never heard from her again.

7. Fact: I had checked into a different hospice several months before David died. However, I found we would only have a nursing assistant once a week instead of three times a week. I didn't change because I feared being alone even more. This was not a good decision. Then David's care kept me so busy I didn't have time to make a change.

8. Fact: In Indiana, I had a right to refuse to be the caregiver. Considering your health and family assistance, this needs to be seriously considered.
9. Fact: If you choose to be the caregiver, prepare yourself by learning skills, asking questions and searching the web for information.

Appendix 2: Coping Techniques

1. When dealing with any disease, do a web search or call a medical library for detailed information. The literature may be dated from the library, but it will be a way to prepare questions for the doctor/surgeon. Some web sites would be, www.medlineplus.gov and www.mayoclinic.com Professional medical societies or foundations, www.medem.com NIH Senior Health, http://nihseniorhealth.gov/

2. The greatest stressor is the unknown.

   a. When you do your research be sure to find out what equipment will be needed. Get items just before you need them. You don't want to buy equipment you'll never use. There are service clubs like the Lion's Club who provide items like walkers, wheelchairs, commodes, etc., in certain areas. Check with them first.

   b. Ask your doctor to guide you for more detailed information or call:

      i. "Nurse Assist or Ask-a-Nurse in your area.

      ii. Social Services.

      iii. Your local hospital.

      iv. Public Health.

   c. Hospital supply stores can help, but remember they are trying to make a living. Compare prices.

      d. Necessary equipment will help your
loved one remain independent as
long as possible, and it will save
your health.
3. Learn to meditate. (Always check with your
doctor before starting a new program.)
      a. Play soothing music softly in the
background. (optional)
      b. It's a simple technique. The hard part
is making sure you do it.
      c. Meditate at approximately the same
time every day. Early morning is
best as it prepares you for the rest of
the day.
      d. Sample Technique: (Takes 15 to 30
minutes.)

4. Dim lights and or pull the shade. Need a
quiet atmosphere. Sit in a comfortable chair that
supports your head. Put your feet flat on the floor.
Be sure you are warm enough, comfortable.
Lay your hands, palms up, in your lap.
Breathe deeply from your diaphragm through your
nose, hold it to the count of ten. Relax and exhale
through your mouth. Repeat three times.
Starting with your head, work your way down the
body. Think of the tension in your scalp, your
face, your neck, your chest, your back. Continue
on with this down to your toes. As you breathe in
say to yourself, *all the muscles in my scalp are
relaxed*. Then do the same with your face and so
on. If you can imagine a picture of the scalp, face,
etc., when addressing each area, it will help you to

keep your concentration, but it won't affect the process if you can't.

a. Another option: Prior to beginning this technique, tightening each muscle group will help release more tension and aid relaxation.

Now imagine your favorite place to be. It doesn't matter where, just as long as it is peaceful and you love it. Go there alone and watch the happenings around you. You will come back when you need to.

When you come back, slowly open your eyes and sit for a moment, realizing the calm that has come to body and spirit.

Thank the Lord for the blessing of this peace.

Go about your daily routine. After a few days, you will gradually become more and more energized.

5. Allow yourself to cry.

6. It's OK to punch pillows or be angry about being left alone.

7. Some people cope by talking about their loved one.

8. Does this work for you? If not, experiment to find out what does work for you.

9. When you are able to read a book, one you might consider is "Heaven" by Randy Anchor. He discusses what heaven will be like, using scripture to support his work.

10. It's OK to get an Erma Bombeck book. Laughter is healthy and can get you through the rough spots.

11. It's OK to remember the good and the bad. They are all part of your life. From every happening comes God's intent, even though we can't see the results or understand them.

12. Remember that "Everything is in Divine Order." Seems I'm always saying this, join me!

13. It is allowed to change the subject when the conversation becomes troublesome.

14. Leaving the room is allowed. Politely excuse yourself.

15. Follow your needs, not the needs of others. Always be polite when doing so. Others are grieving the loss as well.

16. Choose a support group that works for you.

17. The above mentioned services under Appendix 2- number 1. can help with this as well as your minister. The group does not necessarily have to be the one with your church. Sometimes you're better off with strangers.

18.. Follow your heart. Grieving is a natural process. If the group works for you, stick with it. If not, look for something else. If you want a book on the subject, browse the library or bookstore until you find the one that is right for you. The reference librarian should be helpful for this. Sometimes family or friends can offer constructive support, sometimes not. See how it feels for you.

19. After a loved one dies, the family and friends may need to talk about changes they noticed before the diagnosis. This may be their way to cope with their loss.

Appendix 3: Bible Verses That May Be Helpful
1. <u>Comfort:</u> Ps 23.
   Ps 119: 76. Let, I pray Thee, Thy merciful kindness be for my comfort, according to Thy word unto Thy servant.
   Ps 119:77. Let Thy tender mercies come unto me, that I may live: For Thy law is my delight.
2. <u>Love:</u> Jn 15: 9. As the Father hath loved Me, so have I loved you: continue ye in My love.
3. <u>Strength:</u> Ephesians 6: 10 through 18.
   v. 10: Finally, my brethren, be strong in the Lord, and in the power of His might.
   v. 11: Put on the whole armor of God that ye may be able to stand against the wiles of the devil.
   v. 12: For we wrestle not against flesh and blood, but against principalities, against powers, against the rulers of the darkness of this world, against spiritual wickedness in high places.
   v. 13: Wherefore take unto you the whole armor of God that ye may be able to withstand in the evil days, and having done all, to stand.
   v. 14: Stand therefore, having your loins girt about with truth, and having on the breastplate of righteousness;

v. 15: And your feet shod with the preparation of the gospel of peace;

v. 16: Above all, taking the shield of faith, wherewith ye shall be able to quench all the fiery darts of the wicked.

v. 17: And take the helmet of salvation, and the sword of the Spirit, which is the word of God:

v. 18: Praying always with all prayer and supplication in the Spirit, and watching thereunto with all perseverance and supplication for all saints.

4, Abandonment: Ps 86:7. In the day of my trouble I will call upon Thee: For Thou wilt answer me.

5, Where is my Loved One? ll Co. 5: 6 - 8. Therefore we are always confident, knowing that, whilst we are at home in the body, we are absent from the Lord: (For we walk by faith, not by sight.) We are confident, I say and willing rather to be absent from the body, and to be present with the Lord.

6. Peace: Ps. 29:11. The Lord will give strength unto His People; The Lord will bless His People with peace.

7. How do I "Let Go?" Ps 37: 3-6. Trust in the Lord, and do good; So shalt thou dwell in the land, and verily thou shalt be fed. Delight thyself also in the Lord; And He shall give thee the desires of thine heart. Commit thy way unto the Lord; Trust also in Him; and He shall bring

113

it to pass. And He shall bring forth thy righteousness as the light, And thy judgment as the noonday.

8. Despair: Ps. 37: 23 & 24. The steps of a good man are ordered by the Lord: And He delighteth in his way. Though he fall, he shall not be utterly cast down: For the Lord upholdeth him with His hand.

Bible verses were taken from the Companion Study Bible.

Ship on the Horizon

Let us picture in our minds a beautiful blue lagoon
on a clear day.
A fine sailing ship spreads her brilliant white canvas
in a fresh morning breeze and sails out
to the open sea.
We watch her grow smaller and smaller as she nears
the horizon.
Finally, where the sea and sky meet she slips
silently from sight
and someone near you says, "There, she is gone."
Gone where? Gone from sight, that is all.
She is still as large in mast and hull,
still just as able to bear her load.
We can be sure that just as we are saying, "There,
she is gone,"
another is saying, "There she comes!"
Life is eternal and love is immortal.
And death is only a horizon,
and a horizon is nothing save the limit of our sight.
As one door closes another opens.
While we are mourning the loss of a loved one,
others are rejoicing to meet them again
beyond the veil.

Rossiter Worthington Raymond
1840 – 1918

Brief explanation of the differences
between ALS and PBP

Amyotrophic lateral sclerosis (a-mi-oh-TROH-fik
LAT-ur-ul skluh-ROH-sis), or ALS, is a serious
neurological disease that causes muscle weakness,
disability and eventually death. ALS is often called
Lou Gehrig's disease, after the famous baseball
player who was diagnosed with it in 1939. In the
U.S., ALS and motor neuron disease (MND) are
sometimes used interchangeably.

Worldwide, ALS occurs in 1 to 3 people per
100,000. In the vast majority of cases — 90 to 95
percent — doctors don't yet know why ALS occurs.
About 5 to 10 percent of ALS cases are inherited.
ALS often begins with muscle twitching and
weakness in an arm or leg, or with slurring of
speech. Eventually, ALS affects your ability to
control the muscles needed to move, speak, eat and
breathe.

The disease frequently begins in your hands, feet or
limbs, and then spreads to other parts of your body.
As the disease advances, your muscles become
progressively weaker until they're paralyzed. It
eventually affects chewing, swallowing, speaking
and breathing.

PBP

This search was completed August 2011. The
results are still the same as you can see. "We're
sorry, your search for **"Progressive Bulbar Palsy"**
returned no results."

My empirical knowledge, which was acquired while
living this story and from various medical doctors,
shows that the disease process for PBP is the

opposite of ALS. Whereas ALS starts in the
extremities and gradually proceeds toward the trunk
of the body, PBP starts in the trunk of the body and
proceeds outward toward the limbs. Expected
survival rate with PBP is three to five years. ALS
expected survival rate varies. Data collected 2011
from www.mayo.com

Carolee O'Neill

Carolee

About the Author

As a mother of five, Carolee went to college to obtain a baccalaureate degree in nursing, graduating magna cum laude in four years while raising five children. Some of her duties as a nurse allowed her to lecture for the hospital on stress and wellness within the community, counsel the staff and teach infection control measures. After she left nursing, she opened a real estate company to meet the needs of others. Carolee began to write during this period, working privately under the direction of a PhD. Other than writing, she plays the piano, paints watercolor landscapes and illustrations for her children's books and travels cross-country with her motor home to promote her work.

A Reason to Dream

Carolee O'Neill

The Carolee Collectables

by Carolee O'Neill

Goodie RudeShoes: Series One, children 5 to 100.
Billy BitterBetter: Series Two, children 5 to 100.
Granny NeatFreak: children 4 to 100.
The Mouse House: children 4 to 100.
That Secret Part of Me: children 3 to 100.
From Silly to Sinister: Short Stories
fiction for teens through mature adults.
Book One and Two,
Navigating the Potholes of Life,
fiction for teens and adults.
adventure, comedy, drama.
A Reason to Dream,
fiction for teens and adults,
a drama based on a true story.
Three versions of The Graduation.
The Graduation: A stand-alone novel
for teens and adults.
The Graduation with Study Guide
for parents with teens, teens and adults.
The Graduation Study Guide
for those who prefer a separate copy of the guide.
suspense, humor, insightful, endurance.
With God in Mind.
Thought provoking prose
for teens through mature adults.

Carolee can reached at: caroleeagain1934@gmail.com
http://books2c4kids.com

Carolee's books are available as paperback and as ebooks.
Thank you for your interest in my work.

A Reason to Dream

Carolee O'Neill

A Reason to Dream

www.ingramcontent.com/pod-product-compliance
Lightning Source LLC
Chambersburg PA
CBHW070601180626
46817CB00005B/1940